Liz heard screamin̶ː ̶
 the screams was h̶
what happened nex̶
 Maria turn̶

Time seemed to slow like it did in a dream . . . or a vision. Then Liz realized why this moment seemed familiar: It was her vision. Maria was slightly ahead of her and sprinting down the hallway with a monster behind her. . . .

For a moment, she wanted to grab Maria so they could turn and fight. It was what Max would do, even if he knew the fight was lost from the beginning. Liz might have done it, too, except Maria was going too fast and was too close to the balcony for Liz to stop her now. She was going to go over, and Liz was going to watch her. . . .

For the second time.

 NIGHTSCAPE

ROSWELL™

Available from SIMON PULSE

ROSWELL™

 NIGHTSCAPE

KEVIN RYAN

From the television series
developed by Jason Katims

SIMON PULSE
New York   London   Toronto   Sydney   Singapore

First Simon Pulse edition July 2003

™ & © 2003 Twentieth Century Fox Film Corporation, Regency Entertainment (USA) Inc., and Monarchy Enterprises B.V.

SIMON PULSE
An imprint of Simon & Schuster
Children's Publishing Division
1230 Avenue of the Americas
New York, NY 10020

Printed in the United States of America
10 9 8 7 6 5 4 3 2 1

Library of Congress Control Number 2003100465

ISBN 0-689-85521-4

For Natasha, who likes aliens and ghosts, and other model citizens

NIGHTSCAPE

PROLOGUE

Isabel watched the road from the window of the van. She stared straight out, and the road flew past her field of vision. When she was bored with that, she could track a single spot a few feet away and watch that one pass more slowly. At least it gave the illusion of moving at a lower speed.

It was a child's game, one that would distract her for seconds at a time. When she was a girl, she would stare out the window watching the road go by and her mind would fly off to a thousand different directions—all of them fun, all of them exciting, and most of them having to do with the future. Now she was living that little girl's future and all she wanted to do was crawl back into that past life.

Isabel wasn't a girl anymore. She was a married woman . . . a married woman who had just lost her husband. Would she ever see Jesse again? She didn't think so. The memory of him pulled at her. How much of herself had she left in Roswell? Isabel had had plenty of time in the last two weeks to ponder that question. She didn't like any of the answers she'd come up with.

Too much, she thought. Too many parts of herself that were good and full of new hope. What was left of her felt shredded, and the pieces didn't form a whole person—at least not a person she wanted to know, let alone be.

Finding no relief on the road, Isabel scanned the inside of the van. In the front, Max and Liz sat in contented silence. Isabel felt a flash of envy at Max's happiness. He had brought his life with him, or at least the part that mattered most to him: Liz.

Even Michael and Maria had each other. Of course they argued and got on each other's nerves, but that was no different from how it had been in Roswell. Kyle had come for his own reasons: He was running from a dead end future in Roswell. She knew he had come at least partly for her as well. There was a time when that would have fed her ego. Now, she just questioned his judgment.

Her past. Her hopes. Jesse. Silly schoolgirl dreams. They were chasing her, and Max couldn't drive fast enough to outrun them.

Ghosts.

There was only one kind of relief that Isabel had known on this trip, and she felt it tugging gently at the edge of her awareness. She allowed herself to drop deeper and finally she felt sleep take her. She didn't fight it. In fact, she embraced it fiercely . . .

Or desperately, she thought.

Isabel dreamed she was being pulled somewhere. She didn't want to go. She was afraid, but she felt herself going, anyway.

2

Then she realized she wasn't being pulled anymore. She was walking. It was her own legs that were taking her. She was no less afraid, but she felt relief that she was at least in control.

Looking down at her legs, she saw that she was wearing a dress and . . . those shoes. Isabel realized where she was. She looked up again, and sure enough she was on the dance floor . . . it was the gym at school.

The prom.

The room was full of kids from school. Isabel knew that Max and Michael were in here somewhere, but she knew it wasn't them she had come to see. Suddenly, she wanted to dance. After all, except for a few dances with her new husband at the wedding, she hadn't danced since the prom, the night that everything had changed for her.

"Can I have this dance?" a voice behind her said.

Isabel turned and saw Alex, looking just as he had at the prom. He was smiling and holding out a hand to her.

She took his hand and felt the tears come freely to her eyes.

"Hey, hey. There's no need for that. It's tough on my ego, you know," he said.

Isabel grabbed him tightly and fell into a silent, slow dance with him. When she felt she was composed enough, she leaned back and looked at him. He was smiling at her, looking at her the way he had at the prom—and a thousand times before that. She hadn't seen it for a long time. Then, she hadn't taken the look seriously. But finally she had known what the look meant, because at the prom she had looked at him the same way. "Is it really you, Alex?" Isabel asked.

"Do you really doubt it?" he asked.

She looked at him closely. He looked like Alex and, more importantly, he felt like Alex. "But is it really you, or is it me

3

imagining you? Imagining what you'd look like, what you'd say?" Isabel asked. She realized her voice sounded a little desperate, but she didn't care.

"I don't know, Isabel. I can't tell the difference," he said, and shrugged.

"I haven't seen you like this in so long," Isabel said.

After Alex died, she had seen him in her mind and talked with him often, but it had been a while. In fact, she couldn't remember the last time she had seen him.

Seen him or dreamed him? She couldn't tell the difference.

"I've been here," he said. "You just stopped coming around. You don't call, you don't write—"

"I know, I'm sorry. It's been so crazy . . . ," she said, but it sounded weak to her own ears.

"What with, falling in love with Jesse and getting married to him?" Alex said, a smile on his lips.

Isabel didn't know how to respond.

"It's okay. You had to move on. I'm stuck here, you don't have to be. And he seemed like a nice enough guy, if you like that Latin GQ type," he said.

"Jealous?" she teased.

"Duh," he said.

"Aren't you supposed to be above that now?" she said.

Alex only shrugged.

Isabel smiled. "He was good to me," she said.

"I know. I want you to be happy, and if those kind of freakish good looks made you happy, so be it," he said.

"Michael said he just wasn't the one. And maybe he was right. I left Jesse, and I left him because I could leave him. I love him, but I was able to go."

Alex nodded as if he understood.

4

"I never forgot this night," she said.

"Me either," he replied. *"Come on."*

Alex led her to the side of the gym. On the way she noticed that everyone else had disappeared. Now it was just the two of them, alone in the gym. He stopped in front of the punch bowl and poured two cups, giving her one. *"It's funny the things you miss,"* he said as he raised his glass.

Isabel touched hers to his. *"To old friends,"* she said.

"To the future," he replied pointedly. Alex took a long sip, finishing the punch in one gulp.

"Isabel, you know you have to move on," he said. But as he spoke he was looking at her intently, *"I mean really move on,"* he said. He paused for a moment and said, *"It's getting late."*

"What do you mean?" she asked.

"It means I have to move on too," he explained, *"but I can't if you keep me here."*

"I have tried. I don't know how to," she said. She was lying and afraid that he could see the lie on her face. Keeping him to herself was selfish, but she couldn't let go. She couldn't give him up yet.

"Okay," he said gently. *"Just try, okay?"*

Isabel nodded, and then he leaned down and kissed her softly, and sweetly. *"It's getting late,"* he said.

Then Alex disappeared. The room went dark, and Isabel was alone.

Then there were voices. They were talking, calling her to them.

"How about the deli?" someone said.

Isabel opened her eyes. She was in the van. They were parked on the street in a town somewhere.

"Deli food sounds good to me," she said quickly.

5

1

"Max, I'll be just a minute," Michael said. Then he leveled a serious look at Max, who nodded. Something was going on—that much, Liz could see. And she was instantly alert. They had covered hundreds of miles in the last three days. They were in Washington State, and Roswell was far behind them now. When they had left town on the night of their high school graduation, they had assumed they had left many of their problems behind.

A small town on the southern border of Colorado named Stonewall had shown them that that wasn't true. Still, as they increased their distance from Roswell and Stonewall, Liz felt herself relaxing. The mood in the car had lightened, and the spirits in the car had been high— remarkably high, considering that they had just escaped assassination by the Special Unit on graduation night and an encounter with a new and malevolent alien race in Stonewall. They had done some real good in Stonewall. They had also taken on a powerful group of aliens and won.

They had won.

Four women were now back with their families, and the aliens would not likely return. *Now what?* Liz wondered, considering the look that had just passed between Max and Michael. "Max?" Liz said.

He simply raised his hand and shook his head, keeping his eye on the rearview mirror. Liz scanned the town around them but didn't see anything unusual. They were in a medium-sized town, where they had eaten lunch at a local deli and then picked up some supplies at the auto parts store.

It had all felt normal. In fact, it had all felt good.

In the days since their experience in Stonewall, Liz and the others had felt indestructible. Even at the time, Liz had known that the feeling was false . . . and dangerous. Alex had been one of them and he had died. Kyle had almost died again in Stonewall. Liz had been taken by the aliens, almost forever. And then Max and Michael had nearly been spirited away by their ship.

Liz knew they had not been indestructible then. They had been very, very lucky.

She watched Max's face for clues to what was going on. The others said he was a closed book, but rarely to Liz. She understood Max more deeply than even Isabel did, she knew. But now, he was unreadable, even to her.

When she heard the sound of the side door of the van opening, she nearly jumped out of her seat. She spun around to see Michael's face peering into the van. Like Max, his face was neutral.

"Well, are you going to just stand there, Spaceboy?" Maria called from the rear.

Then Michael smiled. Liz turned to Max and saw that he was doing the same.

"Nope," Michael said. But before he stepped inside, he pushed something toward Maria. "Here," he said, handing her a large gift.

For a few seconds, Maria was too surprised to speak any actual words. Finally, she took the guitar and said, "Oh my God, Michael."

Though Liz didn't know much about guitars, she thought that it looked like a good one. It was acoustic and had a rounded back, like one she had seen Maria admire many times at the music store near home.

Michael was smiling. *No, he is beaming,* Liz thought.

"I got you some picks, a tuning thingy, and a carrying bag," Michael said, holding out a bag. Then he stepped inside the van and sat next to Maria.

As soon as he sat, Maria gave him a firm kiss on the cheek. "I can't believe you did this," she said. Then she struck out quickly, smacking him in the chest. "I can't believe you did this," she repeated.

"What?" he said.

"First of all, we're short on room in here. And second, we can't afford this," she said, holding out the guitar.

It was true, Liz knew. They had made some money in Stonewall, but it was disappearing fast even though the six of them had always shared a single motel room at night and they had made sure they didn't spend too much on food.

"*First* of all," Michael said, his voice tight, "we can stow it in the back. And *second* of all, Maxwell and I came up with a new source of funds."

That surprised Liz. And she knew she wasn't alone. She shot Max a look. He responded with a smile.

"What new source?" Maria asked.

"Max?" Isabel said from the back.

"We should have thought of it sooner," Max said.

A sudden realization hit Liz. She turned to Max and said, "You made and sold some diamonds."

He nodded.

"When?" she asked.

"When we stopped yesterday. We picked up some coal and then sold the diamonds I made," Max said.

"That's dangerous. Selling loose diamonds is bound to arouse suspicion," Liz said.

"That's why we sold them at the pawn shop and not the jewelry store," Michael said. "The owner was happy to get them for a good price and didn't ask any questions."

"Do you still have yours?" Max whispered to Liz.

Liz's hand went reflexively to her pocket, where she kept the diamond he had made for her that night a few weeks ago on her roof. The night she had decided that any future she had would always include him. The night he had asked her to marry him. She smiled and nodded her response. "You should still be careful," she said.

"Always," Max said.

"I guess this takes care of our money problems for a while," Maria said.

"We spent most of what we made already. We didn't want to get greedy the first time," Michael said.

There wasn't much room there, Liz knew. It was already tight with the few supplies they had bought, including some tools and auto parts Kyle had chosen.

"We figured the guitar was worth it since it counts as entertainment for all of us," Michael said.

"Well, thank you," Maria said. "This was very . . . sweet."

Max started the van and they pulled away.

"Any other surprises?" Liz asked.

To her surprise, something flashed across Max's face. "What is it?" she asked.

"Ah . . . another entertainment expense. Kyle can explain it," he said.

"I picked up a new stereo. I thought I would install it tonight when we stop," Kyle said.

So that is what Kyle bought at the auto store, Liz thought.

"Not that we don't all enjoy listening to AM radio on a three-inch speaker, but we thought it was time to broaden our horizons," Michael said.

Liz shook her head. The guys had managed to surprise them. And she had thought secrets would be impossible given the close quarters they were living in now. Well, she and Maria had arranged a surprise of their own, but the boys wouldn't find out about that until later.

As Max found his way back to the two-lane road they were taking, Liz could hear Maria tuning the guitar.

"Michael, do you see that black SUV?" Max asked, his voice tight. Michael obviously heard the same thing and spun his head around to look back through one of the van's two rear windows.

"It was on the road this morning," Michael said.

"Before we stopped," Max said.

"Maybe they stopped too," Maria said, with uncertainty.

"For exactly the same amount of time as we did?" Michael asked.

"Coincidence?" Maria said, but there was no conviction in her voice.

"What's the plan, Maxwell?" Michael said.

Max hesitated for a moment before he answered. Just before graduation he had said that he was done making decisions for the group. He had said the same thing in Stonewall. Liz understood why: He knew that, under his leadership his, Michael's, and Isabel's home planet had fallen. And too many bad things had happened in the last few years. Max blamed himself for all of them, including Alex's death. It wasn't fair, but that was Max. Now he was determined not to take a leadership position.

"Too much traffic on this road for us to do much of anything. For now, I'll just slow down," Max said.

Max reduced his speed to fifty. Immediately cars started passing them. But not all the cars, Liz saw. The black SUV didn't pass them. It slowed down as well, falling farther back until Liz couldn't see it anymore out of her mirror.

"Can you see him, Michael?" Max asked.

"No," Michael replied.

"He might have pulled over somewhere," Liz said.

"Maybe," Max said, his voice even. Then he sped up, taking the van to sixty-five. At that speed, he passed five or six cars.

"Careful, Max," Michael said. "We can't afford to get stopped for speeding."

"Better the cops than . . . them," Maria said.

"It's all the same, Maria," Michael said. Then, before she could say anything else, he said, "Look, we don't technically own this van. We don't even know where Jesse got it, but I guarantee you that it's on a list somewhere in every state. I bet the Special Unit's seen to that," Michael said.

"And even if the government doesn't know about the van and Jesse owned it legally, we can't produce a registration and we can't register the van using any of our real names," Max said.

"So even though we escaped the graduation night assassination and the aliens back in Stonewall, a simple traffic stop will put an end to this little adventure?" Maria said.

"Pretty much," Michael said.

"What do we do?" Maria asked.

"We think of something. In the meantime, Max and I have been changing the license plate number every day," Michael said.

Max reduced his speed to just a few miles an hour over the speed limit of sixty. "Isabel, wait for my signal, then we'll need some camouflage," he said.

"I'm ready, Max," his sister said.

A few minutes later, the traffic cleared a bit and the van went over a hill. Even as Liz saw that there were no cars in sight on the other side, she heard Max say, "Now."

Isabel's hand reached up and touched the side of the van. There was a slight glow where her hand touched the metal and then nothing. "Blue," Isabel said simply.

Liz leaned out her open window and took a look at the side of the van. The nondescript faded gray color of the van had been replaced with a bright new blue. The van looked almost new, at least from the outside.

Max inched up the speed, putting even more distance between their van and whoever was following them. "Any sign?" he asked, scanning his own mirrors.

"No," Michael said.

"Maybe it wasn't the Special Unit. It could have been just a coincidence. A second SUV like the one from this morning," Kyle said.

Liz allowed herself to relax a notch. Maybe Kyle was right: There seemed to be no way that the Special Unit or anyone else could have tracked them—was there?

"Liz, do you see that?" Max said.

"What?" Liz said, leaning forward and scanning the road. She had twenty-twenty vision, but Max's was better thanks to the genetic engineering that had created him.

A few seconds later she saw what Max meant: It was another black, late-model SUV.

"What is it?" Michael asked.

"There's a black SUV in front of us, up ahead," Max said calmly.

It didn't make any sense to Liz. "How did they get in front of us without us seeing them?"

"They didn't. It's another black SUV," Max said.

"Anywhere to turn off?" Michael asked.

"No," Max said, shaking his head.

Liz looked around. There was nothing but road and trees ahead of them. That, and some hills in the distance. "We could wait until dark to try to lose them," Max said. "We'll have a better chance at night."

"If *they're* willing to wait," Michael said.

"For now, they don't seem to be in a rush," Max said.

Liz couldn't believe it. This was no coincidence. Somehow,

the Special Unit had found them. Less than two weeks
into their trip, less than two weeks after they had barely
escaped from Roswell with their lives.

"Our friend is back, behind us," Michael said.

That's it, Liz thought. *They're boxing us in.*

2

"Don't worry," Max whispered to Liz. He could tell she was scared. He was, too, but he tried not to show it.

"I won't let anything happen," he said. He kept his voice firm.

Max had given up leadership over this group back in Roswell, but he had also made a promise to himself that he would keep Liz safe and do his best to make her happy. He had nearly failed back in Stonewall. He would not fail again.

Whatever happened, he would make sure that the Special Unit never got its hands on her. She looked at him and nodded. She believed that he knew what to do. She believed in *him*. She still believed. And he was determined not to disappoint her again.

"They're keeping their distance in the back," Michael said.

Liz saw that the other SUV was staying far ahead of them.

"They're waiting to make their move," Max said.

Liz felt a hand on her shoulder. She knew it was Maria's. She put her own hand on top of her best friend's, then turned around and smiled. Maria was scared, but holding herself together.

"Liz—," Maria began, but Liz didn't hear what her friend said next because, suddenly, she wasn't in the car anymore. She was outside. It was dark and raining heavily. In front of her was a huge house. No, not a house: a mansion. It was very old and falling apart on the outside. Then the scene shifted, and Liz was watching as Maria screamed, terrified. Then her friend was running down a long hallway.

Liz had a bad feeling as she watched Maria approach the top of the staircase. There was a balcony, and Maria was headed straight for it. Liz wanted to call out to her friend to warn her to stop, but Liz realized she wasn't there, not really. Still, Liz couldn't help screaming out, anyway. Of course, Maria didn't respond. But even if Liz had been there, Liz didn't think Maria would have heard her over her own frightened screams. In the last split second, Maria tried to stop, but all she was able to do was twist her body to the side. Then she hit the railing and her momentum carried her forward. And she was flying into space. . . .

Then a hand was on her shoulder, shaking her.

"Hey, Parker," Maria's voice said.

Liz realized she was back in the van. No, she had always been there. The other place was just another . . . vision.

"What did you see, Liz?" Max asked, concern in his voice. He didn't even have to ask anymore if she had had a vision. He knew.

Taking a deep breath, Liz said, "An old house—a mansion, I think. It was dark and raining. We went inside." Liz turned to Maria. "Then I saw the inside. You were screaming, and something was chasing you."

Maria read something in Liz's face. "What else?" she asked.

Liz hesitated for just a moment before she said, "You were running down a hallway and fell off a balcony. That's all I saw."

"See, I think this is good. I think your power may finally be coming in handy," Michael said.

Maria's head shot back around, and she said, "Because saving all of your lives from the Special Unit on graduation wasn't helpful?" Michael started to respond, but Maria cut him off: "Like helping save those girls back in Stonewall— to say nothing of your own ass—wasn't *helpful?*"

Liz expected to witness another round in the perpetual battle of the sexes that was Michael and Maria's relationship. But, to Liz's surprise, Michael didn't reply immediately. He waited a few seconds, then he smiled.

"No, those were good too," he said. That got a chuckle out of Kyle in the back, and Liz found herself smiling as well. "What I was going to say," Michael continued, "is that we now have a specific warning that we can do something about. We'll just stay away from creepy mansions in the rain."

"What if it's fate?" Maria asked.

"Like you pointed out, Liz has helped us change our fate before," Max said.

"Personally, I'll take haunted mansions over aliens or our friends in the Special Unit," Michael said.

That one got laughter from Liz as well as the others. Liz couldn't believe they were laughing now, with the Special Unit boxing them in. She was just as surprised that it was Michael who was making them laugh.

Something had happened to him when they left Roswell. Maybe it had happened to all of them. Liz felt like she was more in control than she had been in years. She also felt more relaxed, even though they had already faced terrible danger on the road.

"It should be dark in just over an hour," Max said.

"Maybe we'll lose them after all," Michael added. Then, just a second later, he added, "Police car coming up behind you."

Liz saw Max check his speed. He was going the speed limit.

"He's going pretty fast, he'll probably just blow past us," Michael said.

Checking her own mirror, Liz saw the police car closing the distance behind them. In the far distance she saw the black SUV pacing them. Then the police car's lights came on. She immediately heard the siren.

The car was now directly behind them. It was crazy. They were being tailed by some of the most dangerous people in the F.B.I. and they were about to be pulled over by a local policeman in a squad car.

"Oh, Max," Isabel said.

For a second, Max considered flooring the accelerator and taking his chances on the road. But the VW van was more than three decades old and though Kyle had done a great job of repairing and upgrading it, Max had no illusions about whether it could outrun a late model police car.

And even if it could, it could never outrun the police radio. There would be a car from the next town or the state police waiting for them up ahead. Still, if there was a turnoff—even a dirt road—Max might have tried it. But this road was a long, straight stretch of nothing much.

Up until now, Max had made a point of sticking to small roads and avoiding highways and interstates. In this case, that seemed to have backfired. There wasn't even any traffic to try to get lost in.

Max didn't want to be in charge, and he had made that clear to his friends. His track record in the past had not been great, and Liz's vision of their future had confirmed his worst fears. Nevertheless, he was driving, there were flashing lights in his rearview mirror, and there was no time for a conference. Max made the only decision he could and pulled over, feeling the van shake as it hit the gravel on the side of the road.

Max was glad no one asked about his plans. It wouldn't make the others feel any better to hear he didn't have any.

"I got your back," Michael said. His tone suggested the faith he had in Max, his belief that Max would get them through this—despite all evidence to the contrary. Nevertheless, Max felt himself straighten up, buoyed by Michael's belief, no matter how misplaced that belief might be.

He rolled down the window as he watched the policeman get out of the car. There was only one of them, Max noted. And he was a sheriff, not a state policeman. *Better,* Max thought. *Less chance of him mobilizing the whole state against us.*

The sheriff, who was somewhere in his forties, had a deadly serious expression on his face. When he approached the van, Max nodded and said, "Officer." Max, fighting the urge to say anything else, waited for the sheriff to do something.

"Do you know why I stopped you?" the sheriff asked.

"No sir," Max said. "I don't think I was speeding."

The sheriff shook his head. "No, this is a safety stop. You have a broken taillight."

Max felt a rush of relief. "Thank you, I will get that fixed right away," he said.

"Good, I'll write you a summons for it, but you won't have to pay if you get it repaired in forty-eight hours," the sheriff said.

Max knew what was coming next, and his stomach tightened.

"Could I see your license and registration, please," the sheriff said.

Instinctively, Max reached for his wallet. Then he hesitated. He couldn't show the man his license. God only knew what kind of criminal lists the Special Unit had put his and his friends' names on. And he didn't have a registration for the van.

"Is there a problem?" the sheriff asked.

"I'm sorry, I don't have my wallet," Max said.

The sheriff immediately looked suspicious. He looked hard at Max and then scanned the inside of the van with his eyes. "You kids are a long way from New Mexico," he said. "What brings you to Washington?"

Max realized that it wasn't enough to change the plate number. In the future, he and Michael would have to change the license plate from New Mexico to another state.

"Son?" the sheriff said.

"We just graduated high school and we wanted to travel the country for a few weeks."

"Kind of inconvenient that you lost your wallet, then," the sheriff said.

Looking into the sheriff's intelligent eyes, Max felt his chances of getting himself and his friends out of this slipping away.

"Step out of the car, please," the sheriff said, putting one hand on his holstered gun. Max could feel the tension in the car. Without looking back, he knew that Michael probably looked ready to explode.

Max couldn't let the sheriff run the plates. He and Michael had picked random numbers and letters. As soon as the sheriff ran them, he would see that they didn't match the van. Max opened the door and started to step out. The sheriff took a step back and said, "The rest of you stay put."

Max's brain went into overdrive, trying to come up with a way to make this turn out right for everyone without attracting any attention. He came up with a handful of options—none of them good.

As the sheriff looked him over, Max realized why he had made the mistake of thinking for a moment that this would turn out okay. The man was a sheriff and wore a uniform like the one Kyle's dad had worn. Sheriff Valenti was the first adult Max and the others had trusted with their secret. If not for Valenti, Max might still be in the White Room.

"Turn around and put your hands on the van," the sheriff said. Max immediately complied.

Then the sheriff made a clicking sound and said, "Well, look at that, I found your wallet."

Max felt his heart sink yet again as he felt the man pull the wallet out of his back pocket. They were in trouble now. Deep trouble. If Max allowed this to play out naturally, he had no doubt that he and the others would shortly find themselves in the care of the Special Unit. But he didn't know how to stop it without hurting this man who was only doing his job. He didn't have much time; the Special Unit was close by. He had to get out of here, and fast.

Watching the sheriff carefully, Max noted that the tag on his uniform shirt said Sheriff Taylor.

"Max?" Michael called out from inside the van.

"It's okay," Max said, nodding his head. It was far from okay, but Max didn't want Michael charging the sheriff.

"You quiet down in there," the sheriff said to Max's friends. Then he leaned closer to Max and said, "You all wait right here while I make a call."

Realizing he had just a few seconds to act, Max seized on something. It was more of an act of desperation than a plan. It didn't feel right exactly, but it felt like the only thing he could do. "We need your help," Max said to the sheriff before the man could walk away.

"What?" Sheriff Taylor said, suspicion in his voice.

"We're in trouble. Someone's been following us for about ten miles now," Max said. Right on cue, a black SUV came from the direction Max had been driving. Max was sure it was the Special Unit SUV that had been in front of them.

"Really?" the sheriff said. Max could hear the smile in his voice.

"I'm serious, that SUV has been following us," Max said, nodding in the direction of the car. "They are watching us now." Then Max turned around and took a look at the sheriff, who was watching the SUV pull over with the same sharp-eyed intelligence he had eyed Max.

He's smart, and a decent person, Max thought. It wasn't an intellectual analysis, and Max thought it might be because he reminded Max of Sheriff Valenti. Still, he was sure he was right. Max didn't know how this could all turn out okay for everybody involved, but he felt a surge of hope.

"Don't go away, son. Let me talk to your friends," Sheriff Taylor said.

Then Max saw the doors to the SUV open and two men in dark suits get out. They were in their late twenties or early thirties and had a look that was both bland and dangerous. Any doubt that Max might have had disappeared. He was absolutely certain that he was looking at two agents of the Special Unit.

Max felt the small seed of hope die inside him.

3

The agent who came out of the driver's side was dark-haired, while the one who came out of the passenger side was blond.

"Who . . . ?" Max heard the sheriff say.

"They're dangerous," Max said.

Apparently the sheriff believed him, because his hand went immediately to his holstered gun. Max felt his heart hammering in his chest, warning him of the danger he and the others were in.

The Special Unit agents were almost directly across the road from them.

"Get back in the van, son," Sheriff Taylor said.

Surprised, Max quickly opened the driver's side door and got in. Then he watched and listened through the open window.

"Federal law enforcement," the blond agent said. The agents waited for a few seconds while a car drove past them, then they crossed the street.

Max noted that the sheriff never took his hand from the butt of his still-holstered gun.

"FBI, Special Unit. We'll take over from here," the blond agent said when he reached their side of the street. The other agent was watching Max and the van closely.

"Thank you, sir, but we local law enforcement officers usually can handle these broken taillight situations just fine," Sheriff Taylor said.

The blond officer smiled, but the expression looked more like a sneer than it did a smile. The sheriff's hand tightened its grip on his gun. For a moment, Max had the almost irrational thought that the sheriff was on their side.

"Just relax, Sheriff," the blond agent said, reaching inside his suit jacket.

Before his hand got where it was going, the sheriff had his gun in his hand. "Freeze!" Sheriff Taylor said in a commanding voice.

Immediately, the agent stopped. Then something unpleasant crossed his face. It took the agent a few seconds to get himself under control, then he said, "I'm Agent Spellman of the FBI, Special Unit. I'm going to get my identification."

The sheriff nodded, keeping a steady gaze on both men. "Okay, Agent Spellman, do it very slowly and we won't have a problem."

The smile that appeared on Spellman's face seemed forced, but he nodded and slowly reached into his suit jacket and pulled out a wallet that he flipped open. Max couldn't see the inside of the wallet, but the sheriff leaned down and scanned it for a moment. He nodded, but did not put away his gun, which was still leveled directly at Agent Spellman.

"You FBI boys cracking down on vehicle safety?" the sheriff asked.

"I think even you can see this isn't about a broken tail-light. We'll take it from here," he said.

"No," Sheriff Taylor said.

"What?" Spellman said.

"I said no. What you will do is go back to your car and get your superior on the line while I call for some assistance from some of my deputies. Then we'll all sort it out together," the sheriff said.

"That won't be necessary," Spellman said slowly. "We have jurisdiction."

"See, that's where you're wrong. This is my town, and I don't know you from Adam. I've never heard of the Special Unit, and I just plain don't like you, Agent Spellman."

Spellman glanced at the gun pointed at him. "Have it your way, Sheriff, but you will regret this," he said.

"I'm sure I will. Now, you and your friend run along," Sheriff Taylor said.

Spellman sneered at the sheriff, nodded to the other agent, and turned around. The sheriff watched them go for a moment, then turned toward his squad car. Suddenly, Agent Spellman jumped aside. As he did so, Max could see that he had been partially blocking the dark-haired agent, who was holding something in his hand.

Max's mind registered the device as a gun. Then he heard a pop and saw Sheriff Taylor fall to the ground.

They shot him, Max's mind supplied, but he couldn't believe it.

Max heard a sound behind him, and then he was moving without consciously willing his body to do it. He jumped out of the van and before his feet hit the ground, he had his hand out and projected a green defensive field.

Behind him he heard Michael, then he heard another pop and saw something hit his screen. It flashed brightly, and Max realized that it wasn't a bullet.

He saw the two agents standing a few yards away, both of them now holding guns. Then he immediately lowered the field, knowing that Michael would take care of the rest.

Michael did not disappoint him. His own hand raised, Michael released a blast that knocked the agents backward. For a moment, Max hoped that Michael hadn't killed the men, as he had Agent Pierce. Not for the agents' sakes, but for Michael's. Max knew his friend was still paying a heavy price for what he had done to Agent Pierce in order to save Max and the others.

Max felt a flood of relief when he saw the two agents move. They were lying on their backs, clearly dazed, but they were both shaking their heads and feeling around with their hands. That told Max that Michael had gained a lot of control over his energy.

Suddenly there was a blur of movement, and then Agent Spellman was spinning around while he was still lying on the ground. In the same movement he raised his gun, which Max could see was oddly shaped.

Again, Max reacted immediately. This time, he didn't put up the force field. Instead, he threw out pure energy and directed it at the gun in Agent Spellman's hand. There was a flash when the energy made contact with the weapon, then small pieces of metal went flying and Max had to duck when one flew past his head. He did the same with the other agent's gun, which was lying on the road a few yards away. This time, he made sure the force of the mini-explosion took the pieces away from himself and his friends.

"Everyone okay?" he called, without taking his eyes off the two agents.

Each of his friends responded with a yes or a fine, and Max nodded, keeping his hand in the air. He was ready to act, and he wanted the agents to see that he was ready for them. Maybe that would keep them from trying anything else.

"I have the car, Max," Michael said.

"I'll check on the sheriff," Liz said.

Max nodded, not taking his eyes off the agents. It had begun to drizzle, and it was growing dark. The group needed to get moving. He heard a few pops coming from the direction of the agents' car. That was Michael, he realized. Max didn't take his eyes off the two men. A few seconds later, Michael was by his side.

"They had a radio, cell phones, and some pretty big guns. I took care of them," Michael said.

"Max, I don't think the sheriff's doing so well," Liz called.

"Watch them," Max said to Michael, and finally turned his attention away from the agents to the others who were huddled around Sheriff Taylor. "What did you do to him?" Max asked the agents, who looked at him in silence.

"Answer him!" Michael said, his hand glowing for a moment. The agents jumped when Michael shouted, and for a second, Max saw fear on their faces. "Now!" Michael shouted.

"High energy tazer dart," Agent Spellman said.

Max knelt down next to the sheriff and looked at it.

"He's breathing, but his pulse is slow and erratic. I think the tazer might have affected his heart."

Max nodded. He pulled the tazer dart out of the man's chest. Taylor didn't respond at all.

Putting both hands on the sheriff's chest, Max reached out gently with his powers. He saw the heart. It was damaged. Some of the blood flow had been cut off. The problem was compounded by the fact that there were blockages on the major arteries leading to the heart. Max knew if he didn't act immediately, Sheriff Taylor would die before help came. He didn't hesitate. Max repaired the damage to the heart quickly, then he worked on the blockages. It took some extra time, but he felt they owed the sheriff something since he had been hurt while trying to help them. Immediately, Sheriff Taylor's color began to improve and his breathing became stronger.

A few seconds more and the sheriff blinked his eyes and started to come around. Acting quickly, Max put a hand on the man's forehead and put him to sleep for a little while. They had enough problems without dealing with the sheriff's questions right now.

Agent Spellman said, "What did you do to him, Max?" Max was surprised to hear the man use his name. Spellman continued: "We know who you are, Max Evans. You and your friends." Spellman looked at each of the others in turn and said, "Michael, Isabel, Kyle, Liz, and Maria. We know all of you."

These men were with the Special Unit. They wanted to take him and the others into the White Room to ask their questions and do their tests. Max had hoped that the Special Unit had been destroyed when Tess blew up the air force base. Either some members of the unit had survived, or it had been reformed quickly. "Leave us alone," Max said, keeping his voice steady with effort.

"Can't do that," Spellman said. "What did you do to him, Max?" he repeated.

Max felt anger rise up in him. "I saved his life. You nearly killed him."

"That doesn't win you any points with us, Max," Spellman said, a sneer on his face.

It was then Max noticed that Spellman was bleeding from one cheek. There was a gash running under one eye. Max guessed it was from when he had blown up the agent's gun in his hand. "I just want you to leave us alone," Max said.

"That will never happen," Spellman said.

Then there was a sudden burst of energy as Michael hurled a blast at the street next to the agents. The men ducked in surprise but quickly recovered.

"You can kill us, Evans, but we'll be replaced tomorrow and then the Unit will find you . . . sooner or later. You can't hide forever."

"Let me have them," Michael said. "Let me suck out their brains."

Max saw something in his friend's eyes and decided to play along. "It will just draw more attention to us," he said.

Michael showed the disappointment on his face. "But we haven't eaten *properly* in so long." Max found that he couldn't help smiling. Michael smiled back, and Max was grateful for the thousandth time that when his mother had sent him to Earth, she had sent Michael with him.

"This may be a joke to you, Evans, but there are forces within the United States government that take your alien agenda very seriously," Spellman said.

"We don't have an agenda. We just want you to leave us alone," Max said.

"If you have nothing to hide, then you can come back with us and we'll clear this up right away. We'll finish your *interview*, Max. Then we'll start on your friends. I think we'll save your *girlfriend* for last," Spellman said.

Something in Max snapped, and he was moving toward the agent. For a moment he didn't know what he was going to do. There was no room for planning when images of the White Room filled his head. He found there was something that frightened him more than going back to the White Room himself: It was Liz going there.

He felt a hand on his shoulder and jerked for a moment until he saw that it was Michael next to him. "We've got to get out of here, Max," Michael said.

"What will your friends in the other SUV do now?" Max asked.

Spellman answered, "They pulled back when they saw us engage you. When we don't answer the phone, they will assume we were lost. They will call for more agents, a *lot* more agents. So go ahead and kill us, Max. Kill us and run. You won't get far."

"Take your jackets off, slowly," Max said. The agents complied, and Max saw the guns strapped to their chests as well as the phones on their belts. "Throw the cell phones and guns down *very* slowly," he added. The men did as he said as Max kept his hand up, ready to respond if they tried anything.

"Pants, too," Michael said. Both the agents and Max looked at Michael in surprise. Michael ignored the looks and said, "Pants, now!"

The two men took off their pants and revealed ankle holsters, which also held small revolvers.

"Throw them on the pile, and step back," Michael said.

Max ran his hand over the pile and melted the guns and phones into a single, useless mass.

"Very impressive, Max. We know all about what you can do, you know," Spellman said.

"Then there's just one more thing you need to know," Max said. "We don't want trouble. We don't want to hurt anyone, but we will protect ourselves. Go back and tell them that."

Agent Spellman looked at him for a long moment and then said, "There's one thing you need to know, Max. You have other enemies and other people watching you. The Unit got a call telling us where to look for you."

"Who is it?" Michael shouted into Spellman's face.

"I don't know," Spellman said, sneering.

"Get out of here," Max said. He gestured the way they had come. "It's a long walk to town, but you might be able to flag down a ride."

"You're just going to let us walk away?" Spellman said.

"Tell them what I told you," Max said.

"It won't make any difference," Spellman said.

"Just tell them," Max said.

Spellman and his companion reached down for their clothes.

"No," Michael said. "Leave the pants and the jacket."

"What?" Spellman said.

"I said leave them," Michael said. Then he kicked the clothing into a pile and destroyed it with a burst of energy. Max was glad there was no traffic on the road. Things would have been much harder for them if there had been witnesses to call in their clearly suspicious activity.

"Why?" Spellman said.

"Because I don't like your attitude. And because we were having a real nice drive until you and Mr. Giggles here crashed the party," Michael said.

"Start walking," Max said.

"This isn't over, Max," Spellman said.

Michael stepped forward. "Okay, shirts off now!"

The agents jumped and stared blankly at him.

"Now!" Michael repeated. "Do it or I'll melt you into paste." He held up his hand threateningly.

"I would do what he says. He can be . . . unpredictable when he's angry," Max said.

Reluctantly, the men took off their ties and white shirts. Now they were left with only their shorts and undershirts.

Max found himself smiling, and saw that Michael was as well. "I'm glad you think this is funny, but when—"

"Shut up!" Michael said. "You just don't get it. Now take off the T-shirts."

The agents complied, and Michael said, "Another word and you know what will happen."

With that, the two men, wearing only their underwear, turned and headed back the way they had come.

4

Liz watched as Max and Michael quickly put the sheriff in the squad car. They sat him up in the seat, reclining it as much as possible.

"Are we just going to leave him?" Maria asked.

"We don't have a choice," Michael said. "It's pretty warm—he'll be okay until he wakes up."

"That will be in maybe an hour. That means we'll be lucky to have that much head start," Max said.

"We could smash the radio, do something to the car to give us more time," Liz suggested.

"No," Max said, shaking his head. "What's the point? The Special Unit will be onto us long before he wakes up."

Liz marveled at Max. He had just saved that man's life despite the fact that as soon as he woke up he would probably start a massive police search for them. Max just accepted it and moved forward. And the next time the same thing happened, he would do it again—heal a person who might destroy him.

Of course, that would only happen if they got away this

time. They would have both the Special Unit and the local police scouring the area for them for some time now.

Once the sheriff was set and Michael had changed their license plate number, the group got into the van. And not a moment too soon: Almost as soon as Liz closed her door, the rain started to really come down. Watching the rain, Liz suddenly remembered her premonition. It was raining there, too. Liz felt a chill run down her spine at the memory.

It didn't look good for them, she realized. The rain meant it would be harder to put much distance between themselves and this place now.

The only consolation was that the people after them would have the same handicap. The difference was that they could afford to make a mistake. More than ever, Liz was sure that her life and the lives of her friends depended on avoiding their enemies.

"Like Tom Joad: Doing good deeds and avoiding the law," Liz thought. She had said that when they had decided to leave Roswell. It had started when she and Max had used their powers to save that woman who was about to be killed by the mugger in the alley by the Crashdown Café.

Liz had believed it was possible for them to do that, to be like Tom Joad. She had known the life would be dangerous, but living in Roswell had been dangerous. The thought of making a difference had sustained her when she had decided to leave everything she had ever known—her family, her home—and the certain future of college and a good career.

And in the less than two weeks since they had left, they had made a difference to some. They had helped the people in Stonewall, and Max had just helped the sheriff. But they had been on the road for less than two weeks. Would that be all the time they would get, before the Special Unit got them? And even if they avoided the law forever, Liz's visions had told her that they would all die in a final battle with an alien menace that would take them one by one, and then take Max last.

Once, Max had come from the future to warn her of what would come. He had told her to stay away from him so that Tess would stay and help in that fight. A lot had happened since then, and now Tess was dead. And Liz knew that fight would still come.

In spite of all the moments of hope and happiness she had found with Max and her friends since this trip had begun, Liz felt hopelessness wash over her. She looked at Max and saw none of that feeling on his face. It was raining hard and was getting difficult to see in the fading light, but he had nothing but determination on his face.

That sight lifted her spirits slightly. Maybe there was a way. And if there was, Max would find it.

"Maxwell, we have to get off this road," Michael said.

"I know," Max said, scanning the road ahead of them.

Liz could see the problem, though. They were in a remote forest road. There had not been an exit or turnoff for miles. It might be many more miles before they saw another one. As it was, it would be painfully easy to track them.

The Special Unit agents would know their direction and would have maps of the area. They would also be able to call helicopters. It would not take them long to find a single van on a nearly empty road at night.

Then something caught her eye as they passed. "There," she said, pointing. "Max, stop."

Without hesitating, Max pulled over. "What?" Michael said.

"Just back up," Liz said, and Max did so.

"Stop," Liz said when they reached the road she had seen. Actually, *road* was a strong word for it—it was more like a path, covered by years of leaves and brush. Liz had to struggle to see in the fading light, but she could see that although it was narrow, it was paved.

"What is it?" Kyle asked.

"Some kind of road. Maybe an old logging road," Max said.

"It looks like it hasn't been used in years. It could be blocked, washed out—who knows?" Michael said.

"If we stay on the main road, they'll have us in a couple of hours at most," Liz said.

"What's the word, Maxwell?" Michael asked.

"I say we try it," Max answered.

"That's it, then," Michael said.

"No," Max said. "I won't make this decision for all of us."

"We don't have a lot of time here, Max," Michael said.

"We vote first," Max said, his voice firm. He turned to Liz and said, "What do you say?"

"We have to get off the highway," she said.

"I'm with you," Michael said. Then he turned to the back and said, "What about the rest of you?"

Isabel, Kyle, and Maria all agreed.

"It's unanimous, Max. Can we go now?" Michael said, his voice impatient.

Liz understood Michael. Everyone was still getting used to the idea that Max refused to take charge of the group anymore. She understood. He still blamed himself for everything.

Michael started to open the side door and said, "Hang on, let me blast the chain."

"No," Max said. "I'll do it." He turned to Liz and said, "Drive through. I'll meet you on the other side."

Max jumped out and Liz slid over. She watched him touch the chain on one end. There was a flash, then the chain separated and one side fell to the ground. As she drove over the chain, she watched Max use his powers to put the chain back together. Then he waved her forward and kicked up the brush and leaves behind the van to hide the fact that they had been there. Max jumped back into the van as Liz moved over to her seat. The first thing he did was turn off the headlights. Then he started driving.

Liz was amazed. Max's actions might have given them the extra time they needed to get away. He might well have just saved their lives, but he still doubted himself. Now he was driving in nearly complete darkness on a narrow forest road. Whether or not he thought he could handle it, Liz had no doubt that all of their lives were resting on his shoulders. And Liz knew she wouldn't want it any other way.

It was almost completely dark when Max made his first turn onto a gravel road that Liz herself had missed. The rain was coming down heavily now, and Liz didn't see how Max was even staying to the road.

Finally, he turned on the headlights—just in time to see the large tree that had fallen across their path. The van came to a jerky stop.

"I'll get it," Max said, reaching for the door.

Liz didn't want to see him go outside again. It was pouring rain, and he was wet enough from his last trip out of the van. *If only the tree would just get out of our way,* she thought idly, *Max wouldn't have to go outside and move it.*

Then, by itself, the trunk of the tree slid quickly across their path to the left as the upper branches scraped against the brush and trees in the woods next to them. Liz let out a surprised "Oh," and the tree came to an abrupt stop.

Amazingly, there was just enough room for the van to get by on the right-hand side of the road.

"I didn't do that," Max said.

"Neither did I," Michael said.

"It wasn't me," said Isabel.

"I think it was me," Liz said, turning to see that Max was already looking at her.

He studied her face for a moment and then smiled and said, "Remind me not to get you mad, Parker."

Before she could react, he was on the move again. The van drove slowly, rocking back and forth on the uneven gravel road. Max made two more turns, apparently at random, and then they came to a branch that was lying in front of them.

"Liz?" Max said.

She concentrated and tried to move the branch with her powers, but it just sat there. She shook her head and shrugged.

Max opened his window and leaned out for a moment. He waved his hand, and the branch slid out of their way. He continued driving, and Liz realized they were traveling gradually uphill.

There was also a glow up ahead, in the distance.

"That must be a town, or something," Liz said.

"The Special Unit could be waiting there," Michael said.

"But we have a better chance of getting lost in a bunch of people than we do out here in the open," Kyle said.

Another vote had Max, Liz, Kyle, and Isabel for heading for the town, or whatever it was, with only Michael and Maria for staying away. They headed toward the glow. After that vote, no one spoke for a long time. Liz stopped checking her watch, but she guessed that at least two hours had passed. The whole time, Max kept a hyper-alert stare on the road. He stopped for obstructions, using his powers to move them aside when necessary.

He also made a number of turns when the road they were on ended. They began to see large parcels of land that were only low brush and tree stumps. *Well, we're on a logging road, it makes sense,* Liz thought.

She tried to occupy herself by experimenting with her own powers to see if she could move anything with her mind, but they wouldn't work. It might be because she could not concentrate, but until the tree on the road she had not been able to summon her powers to move things since Stonewall. There, she had been able to hold the ship with her powers until Max and Michael could escape. After that, those powers had seemed to have deserted her, at least until she had moved the tree. The only ability that appeared with any frequency was her limited future sight—and more often than not, the visions it gave her were frightening.

Behind all of her musings were a single thought that she could not shake: Someone had tracked them. Someone had known who and where they were. It should not have been possible, but there it was. And that was the most frightening part of all of this. Their future depended on being able to disappear into the country, to become anonymous. They knew the Special Unit would be looking for them, but she had been confident they would never find Liz and her friends.

But they had found them, and less than two weeks into the trip. If that was possible, then how would they keep themselves alive? How would she and Max ever get married? What kind of life would they have, and how long would it last?

And who had called the Special Unit?

Unable to shake those questions, Liz watched rain fall and the forest go by in the dim, almost nonexistent light of the evening. The monotony made it hard to avoid those questions and to think of anything else.

She was relieved when a bright flash of light and loud clap of thunder sounded. For a second, her heart pounded faster and she forgot her worries. Then it was back to the dull monotony of the drive inside the rocking of the van on the old gravel road.

Another boom. Michael counted off in his head, one one-thousand, then the flash. *That one was closer, less than a mile,* he thought. The lightning was moving closer to them, or they to it. Either way, it pretty much summed up the day for them. It also summed up the trip so far, for that matter.

To his surprise, Michael didn't feel stressed or anxious. He only felt ready. Those two feelings had pretty much defined life in Roswell for him for as long as he could remember. The funny thing was, now that he was on the run for his life, he had never felt more at ease.

And he had never had a clearer idea of what he wanted.

He reached out his hand and took Maria's in his. She flinched and pulled it away, turning her head from the window. "What?" she said sharply.

Immediately, the hair on the back of his neck went up. He wanted to bark back at her. The desire to do so was reflex by now, second nature for both of them. A month ago, he would have done it without thinking, but a month ago now seemed as far away as the day he had found his way out of his pod and into the desert.

Ignoring his instinct, he simply reached out and took her hand again. This time she didn't pull it away, but she looked at him suspiciously. He slid closer and gave her a comforting smile. "It's going to be okay," he said.

"Really?" she said.

"Max will lose them. If not, I'll make sure that nothing happens to any of us," he said with confidence. "Don't worry about them, or Liz's dream. I'll keep an eye on you."

"I'm not worried," she said sharply.

For a moment, Michael had no response for that. Then, he said, "We just narrowly escaped the Special Unit who tried to assassinate us on graduation day. Barely escaped the new aliens in Stonewall. Now we're maybe an hour ahead of the Special Unit, who would love to put us in a cell and experiment on us. And you say you're not worried?"

"I can take care of myself," Maria said. Her voice was even, but Michael knew it was only from effort. She was scared—he could see it in her eyes—but he couldn't tell exactly what she was most scared of. Was she hiding it just from him—or from herself, too?

"Well, whether you want me to or not, I'm going to take care of you. For whatever time we have left, I want to be with you," Michael said.

For a second, she didn't say anything—which was amazing for Maria. Something was going on behind her eyes, something he couldn't quite see. Then a change came over her, and she said, "Is this what this is all about?"

"What?" he said.

"Sex," she replied.

"No, I'm just saying—," Michael said.

"All the things that are going on, and all you can think about is putting the moves on me," Maria said.

"That's not it," Michael said, feeling the blood rush to his face. Why did this always happen between them? Why couldn't they seem to connect, to communicate like Max and Liz did? Why couldn't Maria understand . . . ? "I'm just trying to tell you—," he began.

"I know what you are trying to do—that's the problem. Now why don't you just leave me alone and grow up," she said.

Michael felt his anger rise up, catching in his throat. "Why—," he began, but stopped himself from saying another word from sheer force of will. He wanted to scream in her face. He wanted to shout his frustration.

That's what Hank would do, a voice said inside his head. The voice was right, and that was one of the reasons he held his tongue. He didn't want to share anything with his former foster father, ever. So, his face burning, he slumped back into the seat and slid away from Maria, who was turned away from him and looking out the window again. It was then that he realized the van was completely silent. Max and Liz were staring straight ahead, and everyone seemed to be holding their breath.

Of course, they heard every word, he thought. The van was big enough for everyone to fit more or less comfortably, but it wasn't big enough for privacy. No one said a word that everyone else didn't hear.

Perfect, he thought as he stared forward and concentrated on the little that he could see out the front windshield. He saw that the glow they had been following had gotten brighter. Whatever it was, they were getting closer to it.

Just then, the glow disappeared, and it was nearly pitch dark again.

5

"Max . . . ?" Liz said. "What was that?"

"I don't know," he replied. "Maybe the power went out in town."

"Maybe," Liz said, but somehow didn't feel like that was the reason. She couldn't explain why, but she knew that wasn't it.

Then the road changed again, and they were on a paved surface. They were also going uphill. That was good. Maybe when they reached the top of the hill, they would be able to see farther. If they could spot the town, she would feel better.

Minutes later the lightning lit up the sky again, outlining a building near the top of the hill. Liz could make out only a silhouette of the building, and that for only a second. Nevertheless, she felt a chill run down her spine.

There was something odd about the building.

Then there was another flash, this one directly behind the structure, and for a moment, it was brightly illuminated. Liz recognized it instantly. "Max, stop," she said.

"What?" he replied.

"Max, you have to stop the van," Liz said sharply.

He brought the van to a stop. "What is it, Liz?" Max pressed.

Immediately, all eyes in the van were on her. She didn't waste any time. She suspected they didn't have much time to waste.

"*That* is the house from my . . . vision. We have to get out of here," she said.

Max nodded, "Any objections?" he asked.

A chorus of "no's" came from the back.

Liz turned to see that Maria looked nervous—scared, actually. Liz understood. After all, Liz's vision had been about Maria in danger. Well, maybe the vision would be useful this time. Maybe they could just slip away now and prevent the event from happening.

Turning around, Liz watched the house recede and felt relieved. She barely had time to register the thought when the sound of the engine died. Pivoting her head back around, she saw that the light on the dashboard had gone off, as had the headlights.

The van slowed down.

"Engine just died," Max said as the van slowed.

"You have *got* to be kidding me," Maria said from the back.

"Gas?" Michael asked, as the van came to a halt.

"We have half a tank," Max replied.

"Well, there should be nothing wrong with the van," Kyle said, his tone firm. Liz knew he had spent many hours fixing and tuning the van in Stonewall. "Just try to start it again."

Max did. The first three times, the van's starter just clicked. Then it started normally.

"See," Kyle said as the van started moving again.

Liz turned to smile at Maria and saw relief on her best friend's face. But Maria's smile died as the van stopped again.

"This is impossible," Kyle said.

Max didn't respond; he simply tried to start the van again. On the fifth attempt it started, but this time it only moved a few feet before dying. He turned to the group. "We have a problem here." Liz saw that Maria was frightened and Kyle's face was set. "When the weather clears, Kyle can take a look at it, but for now we can't stay out in the open. I think we should try for the house," Max said.

"No!" Maria said.

"It makes sense. We can't stay on the road when they're looking for us. Plus, the house is on high ground. We'll see anyone coming and we'll be able to defend ourselves up there if we have to," Michael said.

"What about Liz's dream? There's something in the house," Maria said, her voice tight.

"We don't know what that was, but we know to keep on our guard," Max said.

"I'll look after you," Michael said.

"Why doesn't that make me feel any better?" Maria quipped.

Michael winced, and Liz could see that her best friend had hurt him. From what she'd heard of their earlier conversation, things were not going well. In fact, things had been strained between Maria and Michael since the beginning of the trip.

Liz had asked, but Maria had denied that anything was wrong. She'd just said that she needed some time. It made sense. They had all been through a lot of changes lately, so Maria was certainly entitled to some time to sort things out. The only problem was that Liz was certain Maria wasn't telling the truth. Something else was going on, but she refused to tell Liz what it was, or even to admit that there *was* something going on.

"Why can't we just pull into the woods and wait for the rain to stop?" Maria asked.

"They're right, Maria," Liz found herself saying.

"Why does it feel like I'm the only one around here taking Liz's vision seriously? What if the future is set? What if I'm going to take a header off the top of the staircase in there?" Maria said.

"The future is not set. We learned that at graduation. We saw that in Stonewall. Both of those times we changed the way things turned out," Liz said.

"Doesn't that mean we're due to fail?" Maria asked, a frown on her face.

"No," Max said. "We will not fail. We know what's supposed to happen, what will happen if we let it. We just have to be careful. We don't even know when it is supposed to happen. It could be days from now. We may eliminate the problem just by leaving tomorrow. And we *will* leave tomorrow."

Maria didn't look happy and was about to say something when Isabel spoke.

"We have to get inside," Isabel said. "We'll all keep an eye out for you. Let's go, Max."

Max didn't bother to take a formal vote. It was clear

that the score would be five to one, anyway. Max was able to start the van and made a U-turn, which was difficult because of the narrow road. He obviously didn't want to drive off the pavement and get stuck in the mud. Miraculously, the van didn't conk out again. In fact, it didn't conk out once during the maneuver. It also ran fine all the way up the hill.

"It's like the house wants us to come," Michael said, his voice ominous.

"Shut up, Michael," Maria said, squinting at him.

Liz nearly smiled at the exchange, but something stopped her. It was creepy that the van conked out every few feet when they were trying to leave the house and not at all when they were driving toward it.

As they came closer, Liz could make out more and more detail on the house. It was huge, a mansion made of stone with a number of spires on the roof and what looked like towers on each side. The result looked vaguely like a castle, only more modern.

Liz decided it would be creepy even if she hadn't seen the sight in her vision. "It's definitely deserted," she said to no one in particular.

"There are no lights," Max said.

"Could be a blackout," Liz said, another bolt of lightning temporarily lighting up the sky for a moment as she spoke.

"I don't think so," he said. "The whole place is pretty badly overgrown. I don't think anyone's been here in a number of years."

The van approached a short, brick wall that seemed to surround the house, and Liz could see that Max was right.

In fact, the half of the gate that should have run across the driveway was lying on the ground to their right. The other side was hanging on by one hinge.

Max maneuvered the van through the small opening and pulled up to the house, then asked, "Michael, could you give me a hand?"

Then he and Michael jumped out of the van and into the rain. First, they used their powers to reset the half of the gate that was still hanging on. Then he and Michael maneuvered the other half in place, and Max repeated the task.

When they jumped back in the van, they were soaking wet.

"Max fused it shut. The Special Unit would have to break it down to get through. And it looks like that's the only way in," Michael said.

"In other words, you locked us in," Maria said.

Michael shook his head and said, "We'll use our powers when we need to go."

Maria slumped back in her seat.

Max put the van into drive and headed down the driveway—which was actually wider than the road they had been traveling on—that snaked around the main house. As soon as Max cleared the house, Liz could see a number of smaller buildings in the back.

The largest structure was a garage that must have been built to hold a dozen cars. There was also a small house and two other cottages that must have been for servants or guests. All of the buildings were built from the same gray stone as the main house. They also shared the same castle-like appearance.

When lightning lit up the immediate area, Liz saw a tennis court and what looked like a large pool. There was also a fountain that must have been the center of a large garden, which was now overgrown.

Liz was sure no one had lived here in a long time. That should have made her feel better, because it meant they would likely not be disturbed. But the decay made the place only creepier. That, plus the memory of her vision, made Liz want to be just about anywhere else.

Sensing some of what she was feeling, Max took her hand and gave it a reassuring squeeze.

"Wow," Kyle said. "Someone lived pretty large."

It was true. Liz had been too caught up in the creepiness of the place to consider the unbelievable wealth it must have represented in its day.

"Yeah, but why build this out here in the middle of nowhere?" Isabel asked.

"Must have been built by someone who owned a logging company," Max said.

"I guess there's a lot of money in trees," Kyle said.

"What this place must have been like when it was full of people . . . ," Isabel said, looking outside with interest.

"I think it was probably still spooky," Liz said.

"Seriously. What is up with Dracula's castle?" Kyle said. "I think somebody saw too many horror movies."

"And I think I saw this one," Michael added. "It's the one where it's the old groundskeeper in a mask, and Shaggy and Scooby—"

"Just stop!" Maria said. "This isn't a joke, you know. The Special Unit is still out there looking for us, and God knows what's in there." She took a deep breath and glared at Michael. "Besides," she continued, "everyone knows that the first one to go is the guy who makes bad jokes and tries to get everyone scared."

"Maybe," Michael replied, "and everyone knows that the next to go is the nasty girl who yells all the time."

Maria was silent after that, but she continued to glare at Michael.

"We should park in the garage and wait it out in the house. In the morning, Kyle can take a look at the van and we'll get out of here," Max said. He pulled up to one of the four triple-sized garage doors and jumped out again to open it. When they pulled in, the van's headlights lit up the cavernous interior of the garage.

It really was huge, except for some boxes and what looked like various tools, tires, and other things Liz couldn't identify along the back wall. Max quickly pulled the van around so that it was pointing toward the door. Liz knew he was doing it in case they had to get away in a hurry.

"Come on, let's get you guys inside," Liz said. Max was soaked, and so were Michael and Kyle. Liz opened her door and hopped out. It felt good to stretch her legs. Checking her watch, she saw that it was almost midnight. *As if this wasn't creepy enough,* she thought as they headed down a covered path that led from the garage to the rear of the house.

6

Michael made sure that he and Max were in front of the others. He half expected Maria to complain on principle, but she kept quiet.

She must *be scared,* Michael thought.

"You know, we can handle anything that might be in there or that shows up. They can't be tougher than the aliens in Stonewall," he said.

"Okay, your powers work on humans and aliens. But what if they don't work on ghosts?" she said petulantly.

"Max and I have a plan for that," Michael replied.

"Yeah?" she said.

"Sure, we're going to scream like women and run away," he said.

That earned Michael a sudden whack in the shoulder from Maria, but he could see a momentary smile on her lips. Well, if he accomplished nothing else tonight, he had made her smile for one second.

The covered walk ended in front of a large wooden door that looked like some sort of servants' entrance.

Michael put his hand on the knob.

"Why do you go first?" Max said.

"I took a vote," Michael replied, and pushed on the door. He wasn't surprised when it was locked.

Max gestured to the deadbolt lock and said, "You want me to get that?"

Michael thought about it and said, "Then we'll go in together?"

Max shrugged and took a position next to Michael. Then he put his hand over the lock. There was a click inside, and Michael turned the doorknob and pushed. The door opened easily at first but came to a stop about six inches in. Michael pushed and felt a springy resistance back there. Max tried to look through the opening, but it was too dark to see anything inside.

"What is it?" Liz asked.

"I don't know. Something's back there," Michael said. Then he turned to Max. "Ready?"

"Quietly, okay?" Max said.

Michael nodded and, together, they started pushing on the door with their shoulders. For a moment the door pushed back, and then there was a tearing sound and Michael shot forward.

"Look at this," Max said, pointing to plastic sheeting on the door frame.

"Someone sealed this place up tight," Michael said.

By then the others had stepped inside and were looking with them. "Why do *that*? They didn't bother to do anything on the outside."

Michael tried to look into the room. It was so dark that he couldn't even see the opposite wall. He could, however, see a big, commercial-looking stove on the wall next to him. "Looks like we're in the kitchen," he said. "Next time we explore a creepy old house at midnight, would somebody please remember to bring a flashlight?"

"We could just try the lights," Kyle suggested. There was a click and suddenly the room lit up.

"Well, the good news is, we have power," Michael said.

"That doesn't make sense. No one has been here in years. The place was locked up tight and abandoned. There shouldn't be power," Max said.

"Maybe someone's still here," Maria said.

"I don't think so," Michael said. "If someone was around, there would have been lights on when we arrived. And they would have heard us and come to investigate." Still, Michael listened carefully and didn't hear any sounds in the house. He was sure they were alone. It didn't make much sense, but he was sure it was true.

"You guys should check the place out before we go anywhere," Maria said.

"Okay," Michael said. Then he turned to Max and said, "Maxwell?"

"You can't leave us!" Maria said.

"Hard to check the place out, then," Michael replied.

"Why don't we all go together," Liz said.

"Right," Maria said. "That's very important. We shouldn't split up. In the movies that's when things start to go wrong. People split up and they start disappearing."

"Sounds good to me," Michael said under his breath.

"I heard that," Maria said. "Remember what I said before: The smart-ass jokester is always the first to go."

"Guys. Just keep it down and let's get going," Liz said.

They started making their way through the kitchen, and Michael was amazed at the size of it. There were two large commercial stoves, much bigger than the one at the Crashdown. There were also rows of cabinets and a large metal door that he recognized as a walk-in freezer. Somebody had really lived pretty well in this house. *You could fit Hank's whole trailer in a corner of the kitchen,* Michael thought, shaking his head. Somehow, he couldn't believe the trailer that had been his home for more time than he cared to remember and this house existed in the same universe. When Michael had left Hank and the Chisholm Trailer Park for good to get his own apartment, he swore he would never live in a mobile home again. *And here I am living in a van,* he realized. Though he recognized that living with his friends in the van was the first taste of real freedom he had ever known. He had *chosen* the van, and that was the difference. They were on the run, but Michael felt more in control than he had since waking in the desert after getting out of his pod. "Wonder what's in the fridge?" he said, walking over to the door to the walk-in.

He opened the door and saw that not only was the freezer on, but it was stocked from floor to ceiling with meat and boxes of who knew what else. "Someone's been here, and recently," he said.

"Maybe they had all the lights on and that's what we saw from the road," Kyle said.

"Well, it would explain the light we saw, but then— where did they go?" Michael asked.

Looking inside, Michael saw that there was enough food there to last his friends weeks, maybe longer. If no one was here now, someone was expecting some company—a lot of company.

7

"Okay, I'm getting just a little bit freaked out here," Maria said, looking into the freezer.

"No kidding," Isabel said. She was getting impatient with Maria and her outbursts.

"Excuse me, but it's midnight. We're in the über-creepy haunted house from hell. It's sealed up like a tomb—irony intended—and no one's been here for years except that the meat fairy filled up the fridge recently. Oh, and I left out the fact that, according to Madame Sees-the-Future over there, I'm scheduled to get chased down these stairs by the bogeyman."

"Actually, I think it was more in the front of the house," Liz said, smiling and pointing the other way down the hall.

"You think this is funny?" Maria said, her voice rising even higher in pitch. Then she smiled in spite of herself.

Liz clearly had patience for Maria. For that matter, so did Michael— a seemingly endless supply, on this trip.

Better them than me, Isabel thought.

"Look, there's no reason to panic. I'm sure there's a logical explanation for everything," Liz said.

"Why?" Isabel said, more sharply than she had intended.

For a second, Liz didn't respond; then she said, "Well . . . there usually is."

Isabel just shook her head.

It's getting late.

Where did that thought come from? Isabel wondered.

"What?" Max said to her. She realized she must have spoken it out loud.

"I said it's getting late," Isabel said, more testily than she had intended.

Max just nodded and said, "Right, we should settle in for the night."

Maria started to protest, but Max waved her off, "*After* we've searched the house to make sure it's empty."

"If you think I'm going upstairs . . . ," Maria said.

"Then you can stay by yourself down here," Isabel said.

Maria just glared at her.

Michael stepped up to Maria and put an arm around her shoulder. "Stay close to me and you'll be fine."

That seemed to satisfy her, and she was—thankfully—quiet.

"What if we find someone?" Liz asked.

"Then we'll tell them our car broke down and politely ask if we can stay the night," Max said.

"We'd better leave out the part about being alien human hybrids on the run from a ruthless secret organization within the federal government," Michael said.

Max nodded and gave a small smile. "Probably a good idea."

"What if the place isn't empty, but there's nothing alive here?" Maria said.

"What?" Isabel said.

"You know, ghosts," Maria said.

"Come on, there's no such thing," Liz said.

"How can you be sure?" Isabel found herself asking, surprised for a moment that she was on Maria's side of the discussion.

For a second, Liz was unsure, then she said, "Well, you can't see them. And there's no proof—"

"You grew up in Roswell believing the same things about aliens, until you started dating one, right?" Isabel said, immediately regretting her harsh tone.

"I guess we can keep an open mind," Liz said, giving her a strange look.

I don't need to keep an open mind, Isabel thought. *I used to talk to a ghost all the time. Not so much lately, though. In fact, the last time we talked, he complained, "You never call, you never write."*

"Yeah, yeah, I'm sure that any ghosts we meet will be wisecracking but friendly and join our little troupe," Michael said. "Now, can we get on with this?"

"Yes, let's," Isabel said, pushing her way past the others and stepping into the hallway that led to the rest of the house.

"Hold on," Max said, but Isabel continued down the hallway. Max didn't catch up to Isabel until she was standing in the next room.

He stepped inside and started to say something to Isabel but he was too startled by his surroundings to finish the sentence. He was in the largest dining room he had ever seen. There was a long table in the center. Max quickly counted ten chairs on each side, plus one on each end. Someone behind him hit a switch, and the chandelier over the table came to life, filling the room with a soft, yellow light. With the light on, Max could make out more detail. The walls were a rich, dark wood and had candleholders mounted every few feet.

He couldn't get over the scale of the room. *You could fit the entire Crashdown in here and have room to spare,* he thought.

"Remind me to go into the lumber business," Kyle said.

Unlike the outside of the house, the inside was in good shape. In fact, it had been impeccably maintained. And there was something wrong with that fact, Max realized.

"There's no dust," Liz said, speaking his next thought out loud.

"That's right—if no one's used this house in years, there should be dust covering everything, even with the Saran Wrap over all the windows and doors," Maria said.

Just then, there was a bright flash outside that illuminated the three large windows on one side of the room. The loud thunderclap followed a split second later.

"Ahhhh!" Maria screamed.

"Oh, please," Isabel said.

Max saw that Isabel had been annoyed with Maria ever since they'd arrived at the house. The girls had never been great friends, but they had reached some sort of détente shortly after Maria had learned their secret. Now, Isabel seemed to have a very short fuse with Maria. True, Isabel had not been herself since they left Roswell and she left

Jesse, but she had mostly been quiet and withdrawn. This was something else.

Maybe this is a good sign, Max thought. *Maybe she's coming back to herself.*

It was possible, Max knew, but he couldn't shake the feeling that something else, something new, was bothering her. He made a mental note to ask her about it when and if they were ever alone. Even then, he doubted it would work. Isabel rarely opened up to him anymore.

Liz calmed Maria down with a hand on her shoulder, and Max noted that the plastic covering the windows made the outside world look distorted, as if he were looking at it through a fog. It gave him a claustrophobic feeling, even though he was standing in such a large room. It also made it more difficult to see what was happening outside. Well, he hoped they would leave early enough that that wouldn't be much of an issue. With any luck, they would be gone long before anyone showed up.

"Maria, it's okay. There's nothing to worry about," Liz said.

"Really," Maria challenged, "then what about the dust? You said it yourself, where did it all go?"

"Yes, because no *human being* could have dusted a place like this," Michael said.

"Look outside," Maria said defiantly. "No one's been here in years."

Max saw that it was time to put a stop to all this. He raised his hands to shush them both. "Look, clearly someone has been here. They turned on the power, cleaned the place up, and left some food. That's it. No one's here now but us—and we'll search to confirm that," he added before

Maria could protest. "The important thing is to stay calm and not be at one another's throats," he said, giving both Maria and Isabel serious looks.

"Nice to see you taking charge, Max, but as you've said yourself, you are not the leader here," Isabel said. Then, before he could respond, she turned and started heading for the next room.

It was a library and sitting room. Books lined the walls almost to the twenty-foot ceiling. There were also antique sofas and chairs, as well as low tables. The furniture was clearly old, but all in good condition. The bookshelves were intricately carved dark wood. In the center of one wall was also a large fireplace that was big enough for four of them to stand up inside it.

Liz immediately started scanning the books on the shelves. Even Isabel and Michael were doing it.

"I wouldn't mind staying here for a few days," Liz said. "Exploring would be fun."

"And you haven't seen the mad scientist's lab in the basement yet," Michael said with a grin.

Maria was shaking her head. "It's like I'm taking crazy pills. Have any of you been paying attention?"

"Come on," Max said. He wouldn't have minded staying here for a while, but it wouldn't be a bad idea to make sure the rest of the house was clear. He was sure Maria was just nervous, but a quick search might relax her.

Next, they found an office with a giant desk and some more bookcases.

"Look at this," Liz said, pointing to a plaque on the wall.

Max walked over and saw that it was a newspaper article

mounted on a piece of hardwood. The piece was from the front of the *Washington State Times*. The headline read, "Benton Lumber Celebrates Thirty Years." It was dated November 3, 1937.

From his position by the desk, Kyle said, "I found some newspapers."

Max went over to where Kyle had laid out half a dozen yellowed copies of the *Washington State Times*. Several of them carried front-page stories about Benton Lumber.

"Looks like business was pretty good," Kyle said.

"What's been going on here since then?" Liz said.

"I'm guessing that the owner holed up here, getting more and more eccentric, or more paranoid, until he died and started haunting the place," Michael said.

Maria just glared at him.

"Come on," Max said, and they continued. Their next stop was a large, open room.

"It's a ballroom," Liz said.

It was a large space, as big as a wedding reception hall, and very elegant, with chandeliers hanging throughout the room.

"Jackpot," Kyle said, heading for the far end of the floor.

"What is it?" Max asked as he and the others followed.

Kyle reached the bar first and vaulted over it. When he turned to face his friends, he was smiling. "This haunted house comes with an open bar," he said, producing a bottle from under the counter. "Looks like a party."

"Well, we can't really drink, you know," Max said.

"Oh yeah," Kyle said. He had been with Max the first night Max had tried alcohol, and then the second. The effect had been profound . . . and dangerous. Besides the disorientation Max had felt, his powers had gone crazy.

"I respect that the aliens among us must abstain, but that doesn't mean we mere mortals can't enjoy ourselves," Kyle said.

Max turned to Liz and said, "I don't think it would be safe for you now. Not with your developing powers."

"Well, I was never much of a drinker before," Liz said, a thin smile on her lips.

Max was glad for the smile. Though he hadn't intended it at the time, he knew he had changed her somehow when he had brought her back that day at the Crashdown. At first she had been terrified by the changes and the emergence of her powers. Max knew she was still scared, but maybe this was a good sign.

"Looks like it's just you and me, Maria," Kyle said.

"Yeah, that's what I need, because I'm not freaked out enough," Maria said.

"Leave it to our alien friends to spoil the party," Kyle said, frowning. As he looked back at the bar with disappointment, something caught his attention. "What the . . . ?" Kyle said, bringing up something else from behind the bar.

"Great, Snapple," Michael said, reaching out to take the bottle from Kyle. He opened it and took a sip. "That's what I'm talking about."

"What will everybody have?" Kyle asked. "I've got soda, Snapple—you name it."

"Should we?" Liz asked.

"Come on, we can leave a few bucks on the bar when we go," Michael said.

Max nodded and Kyle passed out drinks.

"When we're finished our look around, I say we see what else they've got to eat around here," Kyle said.

"All the better to fatten you up with," Maria said.

"What?" Kyle said.

"You know, Hansel and Gretel? The witch that built a candy house? To attract kids that she could fatten up and then eat?" Maria raised her eyebrows with each question.

"And you think that's what's going on here?" Kyle asked.

"Makes as much sense as anything else we've come up with," Maria said.

"Not really," Isabel said, and walked on.

The group continued its tour of the mansion. They found a great room in the front of the house. It had another huge fireplace, sofas, and large windows that looked out over the front of the house.

Continuing, they found an actual gymnasium as well as a children's rec room full of old toys and early pinball machines.

"I am really starting to respect Old Man Benton," Kyle said.

Max looked at the toys and got a chill. Everything was in good condition, but bore the unmistakable look of age. The house looked like a museum without the red velvet ropes. He wondered what happened in this house that the owner kept it intact as the years and decades passed. He had no doubt that someone had been here recently to clean up. Still, long before that, someone must have lived here for years with the place frozen in time. He guessed that the outside had been neglected for maybe ten years. But the inside was stuck in—what?—the fifties? The forties?

It didn't make sense. And behind it was a feeling that Max couldn't quite place. He saw Isabel taking in the room and thought she looked very absorbed. Something in this house was affecting her.

Suddenly, Liz was next to him. She took his hand. "Feels like they're still here," she said, whispering.

That was it. Intellectually, he knew they wouldn't find any people here tonight. Yet, he couldn't shake the feeling that they weren't alone here.

"Come on, it's after one," he said, checking his watch. They needed to finish and get to bed. He realized he would feel better when they were off in the morning. Away from here.

Isabel stared at the toys.

"Iz," he said. When she didn't turn around, he approached her and tapped her on the shoulder. "It's getting late," he said.

"Ahhh!" Isabel exclaimed as if he had given her an electric shock. She whirled around and looked at him. For a moment, her guard was down completely. She looked vulnerable and . . . what was it? . . . scared?

Max was immediately sorry he had scared her. An instant later, her control was back and her face was unreadable.

"Don't sneak up on people," she snapped, glaring at him.

"Sorry . . . ," Max said, but she wasn't listening.

Isabel led the group down the main hallway and up the main staircase. Max felt Liz tense up and he guessed this was the place from Liz's vision. He saw the balcony at the top. That must have been where Maria fell . . . would fall, unless they prevented it.

Maria clutched Michael as she headed up the stairs. Beyond the balcony was a long hallway with closed doors on each side. Isabel opened the first door. From behind, Max could see that something was wrong; she was holding her hand to her mouth.

"What is it?" Max said, sliding in behind her.

Then he saw inside the room. Like the rooms downstairs, the two large windows were covered in plastic. But this wasn't an extravagant living space, this was a child's room. A girl's room.

Against a far wall was a canopy bed with frilly pillows and a lace bedspread. In the center were a rocking horse, dollhouse, and doll collection.

"Are you okay, Iz?" Max asked softly.

"I thought I heard someone laughing, maybe a child," she said. Then she shook her head. "No. It's impossible. Must have been something else."

Max nodded, but he thought there was something odd about the room: It looked like someone still lived here. It was easy to imagine that the little girl might return any moment. That thought gave Max a chill.

Gently, he took Isabel by the arm and led her back outside. "I think this house is getting to us," he whispered to her when they were in the hallway.

"What is it?" Kyle asked.

"Nothing, just a bedroom," Max said.

"So is this," Michael said from the next door down.

They walked the hallway, trying each door. The entire floor seemed to be bedrooms. There were two more children's rooms—a nursery and a boy's room. There were also a number of large bathrooms and a children's library. Farther down were adult bedrooms, each with large, ornate beds and heavy curtains. Each room was in pristine condition.

"Creepsville," Michael said.

"I don't think so," Isabel said. They were the first words she had spoken since they had found the first bedroom. "It's all kind of . . . comfortable."

"A little over-the-top-gothic for me," Maria said.

They came to the end of the hallway, where there were ornate double doors. Isabel opened them and revealed what was by far the largest bedroom.

The room took up the entire rear of the house. There was a large bed against the wall, and a bank of windows that overlooked what must have been a beautiful garden. Max could see an empty swimming pool as well. There were bookshelves, as well as sofas and chairs. The place looked more like an apartment than a bedroom. Stepping inside, Isabel opened a door and disappeared inside. Max followed and saw that she was inside a large walk-in closet, still full of clothes. Through another door was a bathroom three times larger than his room at home.

"This is my room," Isabel declared. No one questioned her.

Max said, "Looks like there's no one here. Let's go downstairs and get what we need from the van and keep watch for a while before we go to bed."

They headed out to the hallway, but Maria stopped. "If it's all the same to you guys, why don't we take the back stairs."

8

Liz put the last log on the fire and stepped back. Max raised his hand, and the pile of logs began to smoke. Seconds later the fire was blazing, and Max put his hand down.

Reflexively, Liz turned back to check on Maria, who was sitting on one of the sofas they had moved in front of the fire. Maria was looking around nervously. She relaxed when Michael appeared from the hallway.

He was loaded down with the two bags that contained their one change of clothes each and their bathroom stuff. He also had Maria's new guitar strapped to his back by the strap on its soft case.

"Where were you?" Maria said sharply.

Michael's face set and he held up the bags. "Is that a serious question, because if it is—"

Liz cut him off by stepping in front of him and took one of the bags. "Thanks, Michael," she said.

"You're welcome, Liz," he said in deliberate, even tones as he gave Maria a look. Then something softened on his face, and he walked over to Maria and handed her the guitar.

"Here," he said, and then he turned quickly to Max before she could respond.

"Anything?" Max said.

"Nothing going on out there, but I think the rain is stopping," Michael said.

Liz realized it had been a while since she had heard any thunder. That was good; it would be hard enough to sleep without the periodic loud noise. She took her place on the sofa next to Max. They had moved three sofas from the large room into a semicircle and dragged a big Oriental rug in front of the fire. The result was surprisingly cozy.

Liz hadn't realized how tired she was until she sat down. The adrenaline of the chase and encounter with the Special Unit, then the strangeness of this house, had kept her alert. Now, she was feeling the effects of their long day. She was about to lean into Max when he started speaking.

"There's something we should talk about before we go to bed. We haven't had a chance to, but I don't think we can wait anymore," Max said.

"The Special Unit," Kyle said.

Max nodded. "They found us. Even if we've lost them temporarily, they'll be able to track us again."

"How do you think they did it?" Liz asked.

"Did anyone call home, or write a letter or anything?" Max asked the group.

"Of course not," Maria said. "We had an agreement."

"Yes, and I'm asking if anyone broke it," Max said.

Each one of them shook their heads.

"That's too bad," Michael said.

"Why?" Maria said.

"Because then at least we would know how they did it," Michael said.

Max nodded. "Now, we have no idea and no way to stop it from happening again."

"Maybe the incident in Stonewall got someone's attention," Kyle said. "I mean, you and Michael did take a few shots at that UFO, which blasted out of there pretty quick. Maybe that showed up on somebody's monitor somewhere."

"I thought about that, but that was days ago and hundreds of miles back," Max said. "They had plenty of time to pick us up before now."

"Maybe they tracked the diamonds somehow," Liz said, fingering the diamond Max had made for her.

"I think that's the most likely possibility," Max said. "I made those new ones recently."

"But how would they know about some diamonds we unloaded in a pawn shop in the middle of nowhere?" Michael said.

Max shrugged his shoulders. "I don't know for sure, but . . . Agent Pierce seemed to know a lot about our powers, and how they worked."

Liz cringed inside for Max. She knew he didn't like to talk about Agent Pierce and what that man had done to him in the White Room. There were very few people Liz had ever truly hated in her life, but Pierce was certainly one of them.

"They did have one of us in nineteen forty-seven that they experimented on. Maybe using our powers on something leaves a residue that they can trace," Max suggested.

"That makes as much sense as anything else, but what do we do about it?" Michael asked.

"That's what we need to talk about," Max said.

"Come on, Max," Michael said. "You know you already have a plan."

"I've told you before, I'm not—," Max began.

"I know, you're not the leader here, but why don't you tell us what you think, so we can put it up to the committee for a vote," Michael said.

"Okay, I think we have to stop using our powers for a while. No more diamonds. We'll have to earn money however we can," he said.

"That's dangerous, too, though. It puts us into close contact with other people over a period of time," Kyle said.

"True, but I think it's the only way to go," Max said.

Everyone nodded their agreement.

"Well, I for one will be happy to leave this house. Give me the Special Unit any day over Dracula's castle," Maria said.

"I think something happened here," Isabel broke in.

"Why do you say that?" Max asked.

Isabel shrugged. "I don't know, it's just a feeling. Nothing adds up. The place looked like a museum on the inside and is falling apart on the outside. It's like the house is waiting for something. . . . " She shook her head. "I can't explain it."

Liz thought about it for a moment. She had also gotten a strange feeling from the house. But for her, it was more of a sense of being watched.

"Don't worry, we won't be staying long," Max said.

"I'm not sure we should be in a rush to go," Isabel said.

"What!?" Maria said.

"I think there's something going on in this house, something worth exploring," Isabel said.

"Why would we want to?" Maria said.

For a moment, Liz could see Isabel struggle to remain in control. And for her, that was a colossal emotional display.

"I just think there are forces at work here. We could learn something . . . about death. You know, the greatest mystery in the universe," Isabel said.

Liz knew she had almost died three years ago at the Crashdown, but Max had brought her back before she'd really felt anything. Max, however, had been dead for much longer. Whatever he had seen after he had passed still haunted him, she knew, and he refused to talk about it, even to her. Maybe Max's experience was why Isabel was so interested in the afterlife.

"I'm sorry, Iz, I don't think we can afford to stay past tonight," Max said.

"Why not? You're not actually afraid of ghosts, are you Max?" Before he could respond, she continued. "And if the Special Unit knows where we are, nothing we try to do now matters, anyway."

"I really think we lost them, or they would have caught up with us by now. But we have to put as much distance as we can between ourselves and the last place they tracked us to," Max said.

"And whoever has been in here to clean up and stock the place with food has to come back sooner or later. Better if we're gone when they do," Liz said.

Isabel looked around the room. "Is that how you all feel?" she asked.

The others nodded.

"I'm sorry, Isabel," Kyle said.

She stood up quickly. "I'm going to bed," she said. Then she rubbed her arms and said, "It's freezing in here."

She was right, Liz realized. They were sitting in front of the warm fire, and it was still chilly.

"That would be the ghosts," Maria said.

Everyone shot her the same questioning look at the same time.

"What? Don't you know anything? Ghosts draw on thermal energy when they act on the physical world. You know, chasing girls over balconies, that sort of thing," Maria said.

"Really?" Liz found herself saying.

Maria nodded. "My mom and I used to watch that show, *Haunted Places*," Maria said.

"Sounds like a crock to me," Michael said.

"I wouldn't expect—," Maria began.

A loud crash suddenly sounded from the back of the house, startling all of them. It was such a shock that even Maria was too surprised to scream. The next thing they heard was a loud thumping noise.

For a long moment, no one spoke.

"Well, we can't stand here forever staring at one another. I'm going to check that out. Anyone coming with me?" Isabel said.

Isabel followed the sound toward the back of the house, the others just a few steps behind her. The thumping continued and got louder the closer they got to the kitchen. When she was only a few feet from the kitchen, Max stopped and said, "Hold on."

Isabel didn't hesitate, then she felt Max's hand on her arm.

"Let's at least check it out together," Max said.

"Okay," Isabel said.

Max and Michael stepped forward to either side of her, and the three of them entered the large kitchen. Once again, Isabel couldn't help thinking it was . . . comfortable.

The loud noise felt like an intruder in the house and was much louder in the kitchen.

"There," Michael said, pointing to a door on the side wall. Isabel had thought before that it was another pantry and hadn't bothered to investigate it. Now they approached it carefully, and peered inside.

It was a hospital room. No, not a hospital room, more like an infirmary. The walls were white, though they had yellowed with age. There were five hospital beds, three on one side and two on the other.

There was I.V. equipment, curtains between the beds, and trays full of old-fashioned medical equipment that Isabel did not recognize. As she took in the room, she was vaguely aware of Max and Michael closing a window. They also wrestled with a shutter or something that must have been making the noise.

The room could not have looked more out of place in the house, which for all of its dark wood, heavy drapes, and thick carpet was still a place that Isabel could imagine a family living in. Suddenly she realized something and felt a sharp stab in her stomach.

"They died here," Isabel said.

"Who died?" Liz said from beside her.

"The family, I think they all died in here," she answered. Though she had used the word "think," she meant "know." She felt it somehow, with a dread certainty that pained her. Suddenly she didn't want to be in this room anymore, and quickly stepped back into the kitchen.

"Well, mystery solved," Michael said, his voice light. Isabel couldn't understand it. Hadn't he felt anything in there? How could he have missed it?

She felt Max's hand on her shoulder. "Iz, are you okay?" he asked.

"I'm going to sleep," she said. She was looking forward to going back into the master bedroom. The feeling she had gotten there had been good . . . the opposite of the feeling she had gotten in the infirmary.

She started toward the front of the house.

"Wait, we'll all go," Max said, following her.

When they reached the fireplace, Isabel found herself putting more logs on the fire.

"Isabel, what are you doing?" Max asked. "We're going to sleep."

"Oh, just a habit," she said.

Max gave her a strange look. Of course, it couldn't have been a habit. They didn't have a fireplace at home. Still, to her it had felt like a natural thing to do, like something she had done before.

Silly, she thought. *I must be tired.*

Isabel collected her things and was about to go when Max said, "I don't think we should sleep alone."

"Right, that's how the teenagers always get it in the movies. They separate and then, WHAM," Maria said.

"First of all," Isabel said, "this is not some stupid movie. And second, we've been sharing a single motel room for how many days now? Well, extra rooms won't cost us anything tonight. I'm sleeping alone."

"I was thinking we could all pair up," Max said.

Maria sighed and shook her head.

"Kyle could bunk with you. I just think it would be safer if none of us were alone," Max said to Isabel. "Okay?" he asked, turning to Kyle.

Kyle looked uncomfortable and said, "Sure." Then noticed the look on Isabel's face and said, "Look, Max is right. I'll sleep on the floor."

"No," Isabel said firmly. "I'm sleeping alone tonight, for the first time in two weeks. I'm sorry if that bothers you Max, but this isn't something we're going to vote on."

Isabel turned and headed up the stairs.

9

Isabel entered the bedroom and immediately felt herself relaxing. She realized that she felt at home. It was silly, she knew. This house was nothing like her home in Roswell. Nevertheless, it did feel . . . comfortable.

She turned on the lights and saw something she hadn't noticed before: an oil painting in a sitting area off to the right. It was a family portrait. There was a couple in their thirties. The woman was wearing a white dress. She was beautiful, Isabel saw, with long, curly blond hair. The man was handsome and wearing a suit. They both had broad smiles on their faces.

The mother held a baby in her arms, and two more children posed in front of the parents. One of them was a blond girl of about six. Suddenly Isabel was sure that the room with the rocking horse had belonged to her. Next to the girl was a boy who was maybe a year older. They all looked happy—very happy—she realized.

That's because they were, she thought. *Five happy people living in this house full of toys and children and life.*

Suddenly, Isabel had an image of the house as it had been when the family was here. Bustling with activity, with children running down the hallway, household staff in the kitchen and tending the grounds. She saw extravagant birthday parties for the children, and smiled. The images should have been alien to her. Her own father was a lawyer and they lived comfortably, but they were nowhere near as wealthy as the former occupants of this house. Yet the house and the images seemed familiar to her.

Happy children and beaming parents.

Maybe that was it. She knew she and Max had been lucky to have been found and raised by their parents. Their childhoods had been normal and happy—almost surprisingly so, considering the secret that they carried.

These five people had been happy in a way she understood—in a way that had little to do with money, she realized.

Five.

Then Isabel felt a chill as she remembered the five beds in the infirmary downstairs, and she saw the horrible truth: *They must have gotten sick,* she realized. Isabel felt her face go flush and her throat begin to constrict.

Then there was noise from outside. It was her friends finding their own rooms. Isabel knew that Max and Liz would be staying together. And she had a feeling that Maria and Michael would put aside their differences for the night—especially given how scared Maria had been since they'd arrived.

Kyle didn't have anyone, but she thought he would be all right on his own for the night. He was single. He hadn't lost anyone. *Like I have,* she thought.

Alex.

What about Jesse? a part of her mind protested.

But it was different. She had left Jesse and she had done it because she was able to. She had not left Alex. She had lost him. Alex had been taken from her the way those five people must have been taken from one another. What had become of their happiness? Had they died together, or one at a time? Isabel couldn't decide which was more horrible.

More noise from outside. Laughter this time. To Isabel, laughter seemed inappropriate now, given what she was feeling. Quickly, she strode over to the door and slammed it closed. The crash of the door against the frame was satisfying. Immediately, a small thump sounded on the other side of the room. In the sitting area, a book lay facedown and open on the ground, and Isabel realized the slamming of the door must have knocked the book off the shelf.

She reached down to pick it up and saw that it was a black, leather-bound book that read "1948" on its spine. On the shelf above were a series of similar books that went back to 1938. Picking up the book, she saw that it was a hand-written journal, and the front of the book identified it as belonging to Robert Benton. The date of the entry that the book had opened to was March 15, 1938. Isabel got a chill and realized that the room seemed measurably colder all of a sudden.

She found herself afraid to read any further. This was the last book on the shelf, and she was sure it held answers to the questions she had had since they arrived. Answers to the feelings that this house brought out in her. For a moment, Isabel thought about returning the book to the shelf and leaving this room. She could find Kyle and stay with him.

That would be hiding, the thought rose up on its own.
They want you to know. And you need these answers.

But Isabel had decided a long time ago that she wouldn't let fear rule her, so she held her place in the book with her finger and walked toward the bed. She propped up against the headboard, climbed under the covers, and began to read the March 15 entry.

Later, Isabel would wonder how things would have turned out if she had just put the book away. Certainly they would have been different, but whether they would have turned out better, she didn't know.

"Nice big bed," Michael said, smiling. "Cozy," he added.

Maria rolled her eyes and headed into the room's bathroom. Michael had never slept in a bedroom that had its own bathroom before—unless you counted motel rooms. This was, without a doubt, the nicest place Michael ever stayed. It was certainly light-years from Hank and the trailer park.

Maria came out of the bathroom dressed in her long T-shirt. It didn't reveal much except her lower legs, but on her, it drove him crazy. He smiled and raised his eyebrows at her.

"If we weren't in such a God-awful creepy place, you'd be sleeping somewhere else, buddy," she replied, climbing under the covers.

"You tell yourself whatever you want, if that makes you feel better," Michael said, joining her.

"What is that supposed to mean?" Maria said, annoyed.

"It means we need to stop kidding ourselves."

"You are so sure of yourself, aren't you?" she said.

He smiled again. "No, I'm sure of you."

"You arrogant bastard! You men are all alike—and it looks like that goes for aliens, too," Maria yelled.

Michael tried to restrain his smile. "Yeah, it's a real problem," he said, and then he leaned over and kissed her.

Despite her annoyance, Maria responded immediately, kissing him and pulling him closer.

For a moment, the last two-plus years melted away, and they were back at the Crashdown, together . . . in the janitor's closet and eraser room at school . . . in her room when her mother was out. Everything before or since slipped from his consciousness. He was getting lost again, getting lost in her. There were no pods. No Hank. No trailer. No Skins. No was chasing them. There was only Maria, and she was sweet.

Perfect.

The only perfect thing in his life. Probably the only perfect thing he had ever known. He came up for air and said, "I knew you would come around."

"Who says I'm coming around," Maria said, kissing him again.

A moment later, he came up again and said, "You know, about us."

"Don't get ahead of yourself, Michael. Just chalk this one up to the spooky surroundings and the heat of the moment. Don't try to make it more than it is." She was looking at him with her eyes wide and her mouth slightly open. He knew what she was offering, and he wanted it.

But there was something he wanted more.

A voice in his head kept repeating, *Don't blow this. Take what you can get.* He knew that voice. He had listened to it almost all of his life.

But not this time.

"What if I want more?" Michael asked, pulling back slightly. Even as he did, his body protested and tried to move him forward on its own. The voice in his head wasn't whispering now, it was screaming.

"Are you serious?" Maria said. "Who are you, and what have you done to my rude, insensitive former boyfriend?"

"Maria, it isn't that I don't want you . . . ," he faltered.

"Well, I'm here, buster," Maria said.

Michael looked into her eyes. He had once said to her, *Ever since I kidnapped you and stole your car, I knew you were the girl for me.* Then he tried to do what he had thought he had always been ready to do: leave, on his own, with just the clothes on his back. But she had called him back. And it had probably saved them all. She had certainly saved him, something inside of him that was much more important than just his life.

"One night isn't enough, Maria. I want it all."

The voice in his head was screaming and pounding on the floor now, but it was out there. The rest was up to her.

Disbelief flashed across her face. "Hang on here a minute," she said. "Are you saying that nothing is going to happen here tonight unless I'm ready for a relationship?"

"Yes," he said.

"You're bluffing," she challenged.

"Good night, Maria," he said as he turned his back to her and put his head on the pillow. He could feel the stunned silence emanating from her side of the bed. There was a similar stunned silence coming from the voice in his head.

"This can't be my life," Maria whispered.

Michael turned back to face her. "Look, Maria, I've been running my whole life. I've always been ready to pack up and go, ready to leave it all behind to protect myself. I thought I had finally done it on graduation day, but something called me back. That something was you. Now that we're on the run, I realize there are things I can't live without. People I can't live without." He paused and took a deep breath. "I finally know what I want, what I've always been looking for. I want you, Maria."

She had listened to him in silence, her face blank. When he finished, she seemed to be collecting herself, then she spoke. When she talked, her voice was tight.

"Well, call the media: Michael Guerin has figured out what he wants. It's a miracle," Maria said.

Michael was flummoxed. His stomach had been in knots during his speech. Now he wasn't sure how to react. "Look, I don't know if you think this is coming too late, or that I'm doing this wrong, but I know that I want you and I'll do whatever I have to do to make *us* happen again," he said.

"What about what I want?" Maria said.

"I thought we wanted each other," Michael said.

"What if *I* don't want *you*?" Maria said, raising her voice.

For a second, the old feelings came back to him with incredible swiftness. Of course, she didn't want him. Why would she? He didn't deserve her. He didn't belong with her. He belonged with a drunken SOB named Hank in a tin box at the trailer park.

As Maria continued to yell at him, Michael felt the blood rush to his cheeks and his throat get tight.

" . . . it isn't always about you, you know," she was saying.

He put up his hands and shouted back, "Enough!" he said.

Michael couldn't wait any longer, he had to know. He had been patient while they were on the road. Maria had a lot to deal with, they all did. He was content to give her the time that she seemed to need. But this wasn't about time. This was about something else, something more basic and much more important.

Unconsciously, Michael felt himself pulling back from her, retreating to the edge of the bed. He stopped himself by force of will. She was looking at him expectantly, waiting for him to say something. He hesitated, drawing out the moment because he was afraid of what was going to happen next.

"All right, Maria. What do you want? Do you want what I want? Do you want me?"

She turned away. "Michael, everything is so complicated. . . ."

Reaching out, he pulled on her shoulder so she was forced to face him. "No, it isn't. I used to tell myself that it was complicated, but you and I have never been complicated." He made himself continue without hesitating. "So Maria, tell me: Do you want me?"

She looked stricken for a moment, and he knew that he was giving away too much on his own face. For perhaps the first time in his life he found that he didn't care. She was about to answer the most important question he had asked in his life.

Her face softened, and she reached for his cheek with one hand. "Michael . . . ," she began.

He had dreaded what she might say, but he needed to know the truth. "It's a simple question, Maria: yes or no?" he pressed, keeping his voice steady with effort. He held his eyes on hers. Whatever happened, he wanted to see it coming. For a moment, she was silent, and he felt his life hanging suspended on a wire, waiting.

He didn't have to wait long this time.

"No," she said in a soft voice.

Michael felt like he had been hit in the stomach by a truck. As he was still absorbing her answer, she said softly, "I'm sorry, Michael."

He wanted to say something, to change her mind, or maybe to hurt her, but his defenses were gone. All he could do was stare at her face as tears ran down her cheeks.

"I love you," he said, surprised that he could speak at all. He took a deep breath. "I would die for you."

Suddenly she screamed, reached out with both hands, and shoved him. Already close to the edge of the bed, he felt himself fall backward and landed hard on the wooden floor.

"What the—," he sputtered in surprise.

Maria peered over the bed, looking down at him. He tested his limbs to make sure he wasn't hurt.

Getting to his feet, he asked, "What? You're upset that I would die for you?" His momentary confusion was making him forget what had just happened between them.

"Why are you in such a rush to die, Michael?" Maria said, anger flashing across her face.

By the time Michael got to his feet, she was on hers and leaning into him.

"I'm not in a rush to die, but—"

"But you'd die for me?" she spat back at him.

"I would," he said.

"What about Max? Would you die for him?" she shouted.

"Yes, of course," he said, without thinking.

"Let's say you died for me, or Max, or some *stray dog*— where does that leave me, Michael?" Maria said.

"Well, I mean . . . I don't think it's going to come to that," he said, no less confused than he had been before this conversation had taken its bizarre turn.

"But it is, isn't it. You are going to die. Liz saw it in her vision," Maria said.

"She also saw you going over the balcony, but I told you I wouldn't let that happen."

"Let's say you don't. Then what? And let's say you prevent Liz's vision of you from coming true. You still don't get it. You think you're the tough one: Sonny Corleone, the hothead, the fighter. You've practically got 'Most Likely to Die' tattooed to your forehead," Maria said.

"Everybody dies, not everybody—"

She cut him off, tears running down her face. "I'm tired of this macho crap. What if I don't want a dead boyfriend?" she sobbed.

"Maria," he said, reaching out for her with both hands.

She pushed his hands away. "Get away from me. Get out of here," she said.

Michael felt anger replacing his confusion. "You know, this is crazy—even for you." He turned and reached for the door.

"Don't think for a second that you're going to be leaving me alone in this room in this place."

Without turning around, he replied, "I thought you said—" He felt a pillow hit him in the back of the head.

"You can sleep on the floor, Spaceboy!" she said.

Michael wanted to rush out of the room. He didn't have to take this from her, but that would mean leaving her alone. And there was Liz's vision to consider. For a moment, he weighed his desire to storm out against the additional danger that that might mean for her.

It was close, but Michael decided to stay. His decision made, he slowly closed the door and turned out the light. When he turned around, he just caught the blanket that came sailing at him.

10

Kyle paced in his room. He didn't like the idea of Isabel being in her room all alone. The Special Unit might be on to them. And the house was creepy, over-the-top horror-movie creepy.

And wasn't that the first rule of horror movies: No matter what happened, you never went anywhere alone. Otherwise . . .

Then again, I'm alone, he thought. But that was different. It felt different, anyway. Maybe he had seen too many horror movies with his dad. Michael and Maria had argued about who died first: the smart aleck or the mean girl. From what he remembered, they both usually went pretty early.

What about the Buddhist ex-jocks? he wondered. *And what about beautiful, half-human/half-alien hybrids?*

Kyle found he couldn't even smile at that. Isabel was being foolish. If they stayed in pairs, they couldn't be taken one at a time—there would always be one person who could fight or call the others.

Taken by whom? he wondered. He didn't know, but he couldn't shake the feeling that they were foolish to take any chances. Then, before he was aware that he had even made a decision, he found himself grabbing a pillow and a blanket. By the time he reached the bedroom door, he knew what he was going to do.

Out in the hallway, he headed down to Isabel's room. Passing Michael and Maria's room, he heard shouting. *Well, it's nice to see people sticking to their routines.*

Then he was standing in front of Isabel's door. He wanted to knock but he knew what would happen if he did. Instead, he scoped out the floor. There was also an Oriental carpet in front of the door, for which Kyle was grateful. Tossing the pillow down, he wrapped the blanket over his shoulders and lowered himself to the floor. This wouldn't be too bad, he realized. He'd slept on his share of floors, and the carpet here was pretty thick.

Putting his head down, Kyle realized he was tired after all. Well, he felt better about relaxing now. He would know if anyone came to Isabel's door. Kyle closed his eyes and let himself fall asleep.

Isabel had barely opened the book when she heard creaking outside, but chalked it up to her friends moving around in this old house. She doubted the Special Unit would be so quiet if they came in.

Looking back down at the book, Isabel started reading the entry that the book had opened to when it fell:

March 15, 1938

Father would not be pleased. I have not written in

over a week. When I was growing up, I never would have considered such a lapse. Of course, I never thought I would still be maintaining a journal at all at my age.

Father was so certain that every detail of each of our lives as Bentons was worthy of record. Even as a boy, I thought the idea silly. However, I maintained the daily journal religiously—out of fear of him, if for no other reason. Now I am much less afraid, but only slightly less religious in my record keeping.

I'm not as sure that posterity will be interested in my life, but perhaps the children will be when they are older. If nothing else, it may amuse them.

Well, Claire has finished decorating the house. This was probably the greatest test of my bride. When Father built the house as a gift for the birth of the baby, I told my dear Claire that we would not have to live here if she didn't like it—especially knowing Father's peculiar tastes.

And when I saw that the finished home was grand but owed more to Baron Von Frankenstein than Frank Lloyd Wright, I made the offer again. Claire refused. She recognized that the house was a gift for her, and a peace offering from Father. And considering how against our union he was, I had to admit that it was a huge step for him.

"Besides," she said. "It has great character, it will be our own castle. I think it will be very comfortable."

Isabel looked up for a moment. Isn't that how she had thought of the house? Comfortable. Again, Isabel had the odd feeling that there was someone other than her friends sharing the house with her.

She continued reading.

And she has made it so. The children love their rooms and they have spent long days having "adventures" on the grounds. Though I never would have thought it possible, this place is home. I have no doubt that we will never live anywhere else.

Besides, it keeps me close to the mills, which I have no doubt was Father's intention. He has given up on my older brother as a successor, which suits Matthew fine.

Speaking of Matthew, the impossible has happened. He has announced his engagement. She is a lovely girl, quite too good for him, but then, my Claire was too good for me.

My wife immediately insisted that we have the engagement party for them here and has thrown herself into the arrangements with her usual fervor.

The only thing that clouds her joy is the baby's fever, but it has only been a day, and the doctor assures her that it will pass.

Isabel got a chill from that line and thought again of the empty beds in the room off the kitchen. The next entry was from the following day.

March 16, 1938

Claire is marching forward with the preparations

for the engagement party, but she is slowed somewhat because she has barely let the baby out of her arms. The doctor has been here twice today and has given her every assurance, but Claire can barely let Jonathan out of her arms to sleep.

Father seems more and more certain that war will come to Europe and that that will mean an increased demand for our lumber. He is building more mills to prepare, and I have been spending too many long days away from Claire and the children.

That will have to change. I have already told Father that he must be prepared to do without me for the month of July. I will take the first real vacation since Claire and I have married. I have promised her, and she is happy, insisting that we spend the entire month in our new home.

Father was surprised, but I stood firm, and to my surprise, he relented. I think that some of my wife's strength has rubbed off on me. Either that, or Father is finally relaxing.

March 17, 1938

The baby's temperature remains high, though the doctor tells us that it will soon pass. Little Jonathan is brave and barely cries. I thought that Claire was looking tired, so I had the doctor check her and, sure enough, she has a fever as well.

She pushes herself too hard. Though she promised to take the day to rest, I found her busy when I came home tonight. I should have checked on her and will have to come home earlier tomorrow.

March 18, 1938

An incredible thing happened today: Father came to visit Jonathan, who now has a rash in addition to a fever. He favors the baby because he was home more when Jonathan was born. Still, an unplanned visit to his grandchildren was extraordinary. He was remarkable with the other children as well. They didn't quite know what to make of the visit, but they were thrilled by the attention.

I think Father truly is relaxing and that some good has come from this fever. The doctor tells us not to worry. Apparently, these sicknesses are self-limiting and do not last more than a few days.

Unfortunately, it seems to have come upon Claire quickly. Her fever has been high, and her rash appeared scarcely a day after her fever began. She remained in bed most of the day with Jonathan. I think this is the first time in our life together that Claire has stayed in bed after nine o'clock in the morning. If not for the doctor's assurances, I would be concerned.

Now, little Robert has begun to run a fever as well. It looks like we might all suffer together for a few days. Little Sarah and I still feel well. She is quite a help to her mother, as is Robert. I will try to come home early tomorrow to look after them.

March 19, 1938

I came home to find the doctor waiting for me. His face was grim, and he took me into the study. He said that Claire and Jonathan had begun to suffer from skin eruptions caused by pox.

I said I knew that Claire had had chicken pox as a child, and that was when he told me that it was . . .

I can scarcely write the word, as if by not committing it to paper it will not be real. Yet I am my father's son, despite my many attempts to deny it over the years, and I will not let fear rule me.

Smallpox.

I can write no more today.

March 20, 1938

I called Father yesterday, immediately after I heard. His reaction was swift. I have never seen him so driven. He insisted that the doctor stay, and questioned him harshly. He knew for a fact that he and the children had been inoculated against smallpox.

Apparently, the vaccine is not always effective, and no better injection will be available for years. Father immediately called his law firm to find out if there was any experimental inoculation ready now, despite the doctor's insistence that vaccination would do no good after the infection had begun. Nevertheless, there is a small army of lawyers now trying to acquire the medicine. Father depends on his lawyers for everything, and if anyone can do it, it is them.

Then the doctor told us what to expect. The eruptions will continue, leading to permanent scars. A small percentage of the sufferers die, and a larger percentage are blinded. I listened to those words, but I could not connect them to my Claire and my children.

Father was furious when he heard that there was no treatment except for good nursing care. Then he exploded into activity and summoned workmen, who immediately began to take apart the sunroom off the kitchen to make an infirmary for us. By morning, there was an alien-looking hospital in our home with five beds—one for Claire and each of the children and one for me to lie down in while I wait with them.

I am haunted by the empty bed, my bed, in the infirmary. It does not seem right that my family suffer while I am well. The doctor says that the strain that infects them is strong and fast moving. Because of my close contact with Claire and the children, he says there is a strong chance that I will be infected. Father, of course, is immune because of his own bout with the disease as a child.

We also have two nurses, who are welcome because the servants do not want to enter the infirmary.

Claire and I stayed up the night, keeping baby Jonathan close to us. I tried to distract her by talking of our summer plans, but she had an aunt who died of the pox and knows what to expect.

In the morning, we moved Claire and the children into the infirmary. Sarah has a rash now, and eruptions have appeared on Andrew. Claire is frightened, something I have never seen before in her. I curse this disease that has invaded our home.

March 21, 1938

Claire and Jonathan are very ill. They are both running very high fevers and she has little energy for anything other than worry over the children. Because of the high fever, she fears for Jonathan's sight, but she runs the same fever herself.

The servants all disappeared together this afternoon. At first, Father was furious and wanted to have the police drag them back—something Father could easily accomplish. I convinced him not to. I doubted they would stay long. And I will not have people working here under armed guard.

Father and I have taken to preparing their food and feeding Claire and the children. I am glad for the duties. While we were preparing dinner, I was struck by the incongruity of seeing Father prepare food for anyone. I didn't think he had ever even set foot in a kitchen. Yet he has taken command of this as he takes command of his mills or boardrooms.

Perhaps God is keeping me well long enough to see them all back to health.

March 21, 1938

Father and I fell asleep in our chairs late last night and woke to find the nurses gone, and none more willing to come. It is just as well. I think the nurses' growing nervousness just made Claire and the children more frightened.

It has been a long day. All of them are running high fevers, and I wonder how long the fevers can last. Claire will not let Jonathan out of her arms except for very brief periods, even when she is delirious with fever. We also have had to place Andrew's and Sarah's beds close to hers so she can touch them.

At first, I feared for their eyesight because of the prolonged fevers, but now my fears have turned much darker. Father and I do all we can, keeping them clean and applying cold compresses. Claire and the children have stopped eating entirely.

The doctor consults with us only by phone now. When we discussed their temperatures and condition, he was quiet for a long time and then told us that we could expect a crisis soon for Claire and the baby.

Father does not look well. It is not the illness, however. He is aging. I had always thought my father indestructible, but worry creases his face and stoops his shoulders. And I would not have thought it possible, but his hair looks much grayer than it did just days ago. We do not speak much.

Tonight, I saw something that I never thought I would live to see: Father was kneeling down next to the three beds, his hands clasped in prayer. I was too stunned to move for long seconds, then I kneeled down beside him.

Isabel turned away from the book for a moment. She was afraid of what it would tell her, of what the house might be trying to tell her. Though it took her a great effort, she picked up the book and turned the page.

11

"Max, I'll be out in a minute," Liz called from the bathroom.

"Okay," he replied.

Liz felt guilty taking so long in the shower, but she couldn't pass up the opportunity. She had made do for weeks now with five-minute showers in motel rooms with five other people waiting their turn. She had even been tempted to fill up the giant, claw-footed tub and soak, but Max was waiting for her—though not because he wanted to get into the shower. . . .

Liz slipped on her black nightgown. She and Maria had bought identical ones two nights ago, not knowing when they would get the chance to use them since they were always crowded into a single motel room.

From the look of things between Maria and Michael lately, Liz didn't think Michael would be seeing Maria's tonight. But then again, Liz had been surprised when Maria had bought it, considering how things had been between her and Michael. Well, Max was going to get his surprise right now, Liz thought as she ran a brush through her hair and checked it in the mirror.

Looking down at the sink, Liz saw brand-new hand soap. There had been unopened soap in the bath, as well as shampoo and conditioner. Like the food in the kitchen, it made her nervous. Someone had taken pains to stock the house, and for all they knew, people would be moving in tomorrow morning.

As long as they don't show up tonight, Liz thought, giving herself one last check in the mirror. She and Max would be sharing a bed—in a private room—for the first time since they'd left Roswell. She didn't intend to waste it.

She opened the door and stepped into the bedroom. Max was lying on the bed in the dim light of a bedside lamp. He didn't even raise an eyebrow at seeing her outfit. Well, she could play it cool too. She didn't say anything and bent down to rummage through her bag for a moment. Then she got up and casually walked over to the bed.

Max was sitting up against the headboard and it looked like he hadn't moved since she had left to go into the shower.

"Max?" she finally said, leaning closer to get a better look at him in the low light. Although he was sitting up and looked alert, his eyes were closed and he was sound asleep.

Liz shook her head. He had responded to her maybe a minute ago, when she had called out from the bathroom. Still, she knew he was a heavy sleeper, and he seemed to be able to go right to sleep even when worry made it difficult for her.

For a moment, she considered shaking him, but decided against being selfish. After the day they'd had, Max was more than entitled to some rest. Besides, there was no way to know what tomorrow would bring.

Liz slipped his jeans and shirt off, knowing it would take more than that to wake him. Then she pulled the quilt up to his shoulders.

Well, Max will have to get his surprise another time, she thought.

Isabel saw that the handwriting on the next page was ragged, as if the man who had written it was shaky. There was no date on top.

I knew something was wrong when I woke. I fell asleep with my head on Claire's lap while she held our baby in her arms. I woke slowly, then started up when I realized that something was different.

I had been dreaming of a fire, no doubt because of the heat from my wife's fever. Then the fire in my dreams went out. The change woke me and, for a wonderful moment, I thought her fever had broken. I felt a brief swell of joy. My wife would be well, everything would be all right.

Then I realized something was wrong. The fever was gone, but she was cold, and so was our child. I frantically tried to wake them, raving as I did. My sounds woke Father, who came quickly. He checked them both, and his face was stricken.

He put his arms around me for the first time in my living memory and said, "They're gone, son."

I pushed him away, still raving. He had to fix this, I screamed. He could make calls. He had doctors, lawyers. He needed to pay someone, do something. I was mad, and in my madness I could only think that Father had never failed at anything in his life. The world seemed to bend to his will. There was nothing he could not do.

He let me rave and then gently laid me down next to my Claire and our Jonathan. Father made calls. Men came. They wore masks and wanted to take Claire and Jonathan from me.

I would not let them. I told them that Father would fix it.

They waited. Finally I let them take my wife and son. They were gone, and I was in a world I did not understand.

The next entry also had no date.

This morning I tended Andrew and Sarah while I was vaguely aware that Father was making calls and some sort of arrangements. For a moment I was grateful that the fever had kept Andrew and Sarah from waking, for long I am a coward. I did not know how I would answer them if they asked for their mother.

Sarah, woke briefly and looked at me for a moment of complete clarity and said, "Daddy, I'm thirsty."

She could not sit up, so I propped her head with pillows and fed her water with a spoon. She looked at me for one wonderful moment and said, "Thank you, Daddy."

She passed in the night.

I did not rave this time. Father called the same men again, and they came in their protective masks. I wanted to tell them they didn't need their masks. This terrible disease only took women and children . . . my woman and my children. But I found that I could not speak.

I did not let them take Sarah for hours—not because I thought Father would fix this or God would take it back, but because I could not make my hands release her.

Later, Claire came to speak to me when Father was out. I was surprised, but she told me she would explain everything. She said she could only stay a little while. She just wanted me to know that everything was going to be all right. Next time, she would stay longer and bring Jonathan with her.

Andrew is worse. He wakes briefly sometimes, but by now I know the signs. Claire stopped in with Jonathan to tell me not to worry. I cannot help it, but felt better when she gave me Jonathan to hold.

I was glad to see them both free of the sickness. They are fully recovered now. Though I begged her, she said they could not stay long. She kissed me and said, "It's getting late." Then she left before Father returned.

Later, I gave Andrew some water with a spoon, then—God forgive me—I drank from the same spoon. I know now that God has only made me wait to become sick so that I could take care of my family.

But I do not think I can wait anymore.

Father came in as I was doing it and screamed from across the room. He ripped the spoon from my hand and looked at me with a crazed, furious expression on his face. I thought for a moment that he might strike me, then he broke down in front of me. "No, not you," he said, tears running down his face.

He was in such pain that I had to tell him that Claire had been to see me and brought Jonathan. She had told me that everything was going to be all right.

I shared Andrew's spoon again when Father was out.

I know Claire told me not to worry, but I could not help it. I climbed into Andrew's bed, hoping that if I kept him near me and kept awake, he would be well. I lay with him for hours and tried to will him to get well.

In the end, I failed. I fell asleep, and in the morning he was gone.

All of them, gone.

Not even Claire could console me, even though she brought Jonathan and Sarah to visit me. I begged her to stay, but she had to leave when Father came back with the men who wanted to take Andrew from me.

I told them to go away. They had taken the others,

but I would not let them take my son. I was determined not to let them. But I failed again. As it grew dark, I fell asleep. They must have taken him then.

Claire visited me while I slept. She had all of the children with her. We played as a family, as we had planned to do in the summer.

When I woke it was just Father and I. He does not look well. When did Father get so old? I did not think it was possible. He seemed beyond such things, immune.

Father tried to get me to leave the infirmary, but I refused. I still feel well, but I know that I must be sick. Claire and the children became sick, how could I be spared? So I lay in the last bed, the only one that had not been used.

Father cleaned and brought me food. He would leave me only briefly to make calls. I wish he would leave me alone. Claire and the children can only come when he is gone.

My brother Matthew came to visit today. He came all the way from one of his trips to Africa. Father embraced him when he arrived, and I do not think he knew what to do.

I tried to call for Claire and the children, who are so fond of their uncle Matthew, but they did not come. Perhaps later.

Father and Matthew tried to get me to get dressed. They wanted me to attend a service of some kind. It was not like Father. To my knowledge, he had not seen the inside of a church since he was married to my mother. I refused to go. I explained to Father that I had spent entirely too much time away from my family. In fact, I had decided to take my vacation early and he would have to learn to do without me in the mills for some time.

I was ready for a fight. I know how stubborn Father can be, but I was determined, and I have some of Father's resolve myself. So Father and Matthew went to the service without me.

I was glad to be alone. Claire and the children came for a nice, long visit. Claire convinced me to leave the infirmary. I did not want to go, but she explained that it made the children nervous to be there, so I agreed.

Upstairs, we all gathered in the master bedroom. I made a fire, and Claire and I played with the children. Later, we put the children to sleep in their own beds and Claire and I were alone for the first time in too long.

She had something to ask me, and I could tell that it pained her. She told me I had to let her and the children go. For the first time in our marriage, I was angry with her. Her request was ridiculous. She was as bad as my father. I told her we needed to spend *more* time together as a family.

She tried to bring it up again later, but I would not have it. I did not think it was possible, but I had to deny my wife something she wanted. She has asked for so little from me in the past and it pained me to do it, but I had to be firm.

Matthew and Father returned that night. To my surprise, Matthew said he would be staying for a while. He wanted to spend time with me. He would also take on more responsibilities at the mills. I'm sure that pleased Father, though he doesn't show it.

Unfortunately, they want to stay at the house. I only hope they don't stay too long. Claire and the children still won't come when they are around.

After that, there were perhaps two dozen undated entries. He began dating them again in the 1950s. Most of his writing detailed the time he spent with his wife and children, who never aged or changed. The later entries were disjointed and hard to follow.

Isabel felt a sinking in her chest, imagining the man wandering his house for decades with only his memories of his wife and children for company. He never returned to work. Eventually his father and brother moved out and would come by for regular visits to bring him food and clean up. As far as Isabel could tell, he never left the house as the years went by. Soon, there were only a few entries per year, then a few per decade.

The house had been haunted for nearly fifty years, but not by ghosts—by a man who had lost everything and everyone.

The final entry was dated 1988, just a year after Isabel, Michael, and her brother climbed out of their pods. The entry was short and the handwriting barely legible.

I think the sickness has finally come for me. I knew it would. Lately, Claire does everything for me and will not let me do anything for myself. Fortunately, the children are a great help to her.

"It is only fair, you took care of all of us," she said.

When I finish this, I will put my book on the shelf with the others. Father will be pleased that I have completed this part of our family history.

Father visits regularly now, and the children are always happy to see him. He looks well, not like he did when the children were sick. This time has made him a better father and grandfather. He also seems happy.

He and I have wonderful discussions about everything from the family business to politics. He still thinks that war will be coming soon and that the mills will be able to help in the effort. I think he's right, but I told him that I am not ready to end my vacation. Work will have to wait; a man's family must come first.

Now I must go to the infirmary, which I have not visited in some time. Claire and the children said they will take care of me, and Father will be there too, of course.

It's getting late.

Isabel stared at the last sentence for a long time.

12

Isabel finally closed the book and put it back on the shelf, but she could not shut the images of the family from her mind, especially Robert, who lived here, alone, until his eighties.

She felt a tightening and then a lurching in her throat and fought it down.

Had Claire and the children remained in the house somehow? Or part of them, at least? What about now? She felt she and her friends were not alone in the house, that it was not empty—at least not completely.

Was it Robert Benton and his family? Or some part of them they had left behind? And were they trying to tell her something? She had felt something odd when they arrived. The house had felt familiar . . . and *comfortable.*

Had they been communicating with her? And what about the journal? That particular book had fallen off the shelf, and it had opened to the first day the family got sick.

And then there was the strange behavior of the van—cutting out when they tried to leave, but working fine when they decided to head for the house and stay the night. But why bring them here? Why show her the book? Did the Bentons want something from them, or from her? What could it be?

It all sounded crazy, even in her own head, but there were things going on here she could not explain—feelings she could not explain.

And what did Robert Benton mean when he wrote, "It's getting late." Alex had said that to her in her dream. Remembering that dream gave Isabel a fresh run of chills. She had tried not to think about it. Was Alex really making contact with her? Or was she just imagining things?

Like Robert Benton, she thought. He imagined his family. Day after day, year after year, then decade after decade. For almost fifty years he had roamed this house—haunted it, really—driven mad by his loss. Except Isabel wasn't sure he was mad. In fact she was sure he wasn't—at least not completely.

She was sure he had felt something of his lost wife and children. It might have been as simple as the lingering feeling you had for someone you had dreamed about before you woke. Or had they been here in a more real way?

And Isabel could make contact with people as they dreamed. Maybe she was in some kind of contact with the Bentons. Maybe she was in some kind of contact with Alex, for that matter. But what then?

Isabel wracked her brain for the ghost stories she had read and the movies she had seen. Spirits sometimes tried to find peace by pointing out their killer if they were murdered, but the Bentons had died from disease over fifty years ago.

Some ghosts were malevolent, wanting to harm the living. In one story she had read, the ghost had driven a woman to suicide so her spirit would stay in their house, but that didn't fit here. The Bentons were a normal family. For all their wealth, they were a happy, normal family.

Like we were, she thought.

Isabel thought of her childhood, the happiness she and Max had found with their adopted parents. For years, even their great secret was only an occasional worry, blotted out by the family life. That life was what she wanted to have with Jesse. Something normal, something good.

Maybe it was too much for her to hope for, with Jesse or with anyone else. Now she had lost him, as well as Mom and Dad. It was only she and Max now, just like they were when they first crawled out of the pods and into the desert.

Was that why Robert Benton had shown her his book? Did he think she might understand his loss, if only in some small way?

There were too many questions for her to answer tonight. She felt drained by what she had read. Isabel laid her head down on the bed that Robert and Claire Benton had shared half a century before . . .

. . . and heard a noise.

Footsteps in the hallway, then laughter. Her first thought was that her brother and friends had to keep it down. People were trying to sleep. Then she realized that the laughter sounded more like . . . a child's. When she heard it again, she was sure: It was a little girl.

Immediately, Isabel was on her feet. She slipped on her shoes and was glad that she had never undressed for bed.

She heard running, and then she was opening her own door and looking down the hallway. No one was there.

Well, no one but Kyle, she thought, looking down and seeing him asleep in front of her door. *He's keeping an eye on me,* she realized. The gesture was sweet, but unnecessary. She was more than capable of defending herself.

Quickly she stepped over Kyle, careful not to wake him. Then she walked down the hallway, following the sound of the laughter and footsteps. She heard creaking and saw that one of the bedroom doors was slightly open. It was the first room they had seen. She knew this had been Sarah Benton's room. Isabel also knew that when she had left the room she had closed the door.

Now the door was half open. Laughter was coming from inside the room. No, not laughter, giggling, Isabel corrected herself. Without hesitation, Isabel pushed the door all the way open, stepped inside, and scanned the room in the dim light that came from the hallway.

There was nothing there.

Isabel flipped the switch on the wall, and suddenly the room was bathed in light. Her eyes adjusted quickly, and when they did, they confirmed what she had seen before: The room was empty. However, the rocking horse was now gently moving back and forth.

That could be because of the breeze I created when I opened the door, she thought. But she immediately dismissed the notion. She was nearly certain that the rocking horse had been still when she'd first stepped into the room, but more than that, she felt a presence. Someone had set the horse in motion, and that someone was still in the room.

Isabel opened the closet. She got a chill when she saw

the little girl's clothes there: frilly dresses, nightgowns, and casual play clothes of different kinds. *Sarah's clothes.* She looked at the artifacts from more than half a century before and saw Sarah's life as clearly as she could see her own childhood. This girl had worn these clothes, played with the dolls in this room, and she had loved her parents.

And then she'd died in this house, Isabel thought. Her stomach seized when she thought of how this little girl had died. She was third, after her mother and baby brother. It was too horrible, and Isabel turned away from the clothes and stepped out of the closet. Next she bent down to check under the bed. There was nothing there. She heard laughter behind her and whipped around.

Nothing.

If this is one of my friends . . . , Isabel thought. *If this is someone's idea of a joke . . .*

But it was not a joke, and the sounds were not made by any of her friends. Impossible as it might seem, a little girl named Sarah who had lived and died in this house fifty years before was making them.

It was impossible—completely impossible, she knew. She also knew it was true. "Sarah?" she said, keeping her voice soft.

There was no response. Isabel looked out into the hallway. She didn't see anything in the dim light. Then there was the laughter again, from behind her in the room.

A smile crossed Isabel's lips. *It's a game,* she thought.

The soft, nearly inaudible laughter continued. Somehow, Isabel knew it would not stop until she turned around. The smile still on her lips, Isabel got ready to quickly peek back into the room, when her ears picked up another sound.

"Isabel . . . ," a voice said, from the direction of the staircase. The sound of her own name jolted her, much more than the laughter of a girl who had been gone from the earth for more than sixty years.

She also realized that at the exact moment that someone spoke her name, the laughter behind her stopped, as if the voice had startled Sarah as well.

"Isabel," the voice repeated.

"Yes?" Isabel called, starting out the door.

It was probably Max or one of the others looking for her. The voice sounded familiar, but it was hard to be sure. She walked quickly to the balcony.

Looking down, into the dim light provided by the dying fire, she saw a hunched figure dash into the shadows. For a second, she thought she was looking at Robert Benton, who was still alive and roaming the house. But for reasons she could not explain, she was certain that the last entry he had made in his journal upstairs was made on the last day of his life—more than ten years ago.

She glanced quickly back down the hallway, to Sarah's room, and then beyond, where her friends were sleeping. For a moment, she had an urge to go back and wake up Max and Michael, but she didn't want to waste time explaining what she was feeling, knowing they might not believe her—even if they somehow understood.

So she headed to the top of the stairs and then down to the main floor. Once there, she called out, "Hello." There was no response, then she called out softly, "Robert? Robert Benton?" She felt silly for a moment, calling out to someone long gone, but she knew what she felt.

Another flash of movement. She saw the same figure disappear into the rear of the house, and this time she saw him more clearly. He was wearing some type of a hood, and he looked small . . . or was it just that he was hunched over?

Well, Isabel was going to find out once and for all what was going on in this house. If the Bentons were somehow behind this, then there was a reason. Maybe they needed something from her. Maybe she could help them.

Isabel headed into the hallway, past the dining room. And then she caught another glimpse of the hooded figure as he disappeared into the kitchen. Isabel started running. She wouldn't let this go another second. Whatever was going on in this house, she would know right now.

When she reached the kitchen, she saw a door swing open and the figure dash into it. The door was next to a large walk-in pantry, and Isabel realized she and her friends had forgotten something important when they had quickly searched the house.

The basement, she thought. She reached for the door, opened it, and looked down into complete darkness. *Well, that makes sense,* she thought. *If I'm chasing a ghost, he wouldn't need lights.* She did, though, and hit the switch next to the wall. A bare bulb above her lit up, and she could see lights come on at the bottom of the stairs. The basement came into view as she descended. There were no surprises there. It was a large space full of indoor and outdoor furniture, as well as tools and other equipment. Unlike the rest of the inside of the house, the basement looked old. Time had not stopped here. Things had rusted and decayed.

She smelled dust, mildew, and something else she could not place. It was unpleasant, whatever it was. Isabel was ready to search the maze of junk when she heard a door creak. The sound came from behind the ancient-looking boiler, which stood in front of an old wooden door, hanging half open. She opened the door and peered inside. There were stairs leading down to a brightly lit space, some sort of a sub-basement. From what she could see, the space looked clean, as if it had been very well maintained.

She felt a tinge of nervousness. Isabel brushed it aside. She sensed that even if this house was full of spirits, they were good. Whatever they might want from her, they meant her no harm.

Unless it's like that ghost story. Unless they're trying to trick you, her mind warned. There was a crawling sensation on the back of her neck, as if she was being watched. She turned around quickly and couldn't see anyone there. Isabel started to call out, but found that she didn't want to break the silence around her.

She turned and took the first step down the stairs. The sound of her foot on the step suddenly seemed very loud to her, and she considered turning around now and waking up Max and Michael. Again, she decided not to. She would solve this herself. This wasn't a movie, and she wasn't a moron in a nightshirt rushing into the arms of the ax murderer in the basement.

Isabel flexed her hand, feeling her powers coalesce around and inside of her. She was more than able to defend herself against anything. If there were good spirits here, she would try to find out what they wanted. If there was something else here—something darker—she could handle that, too.

Isabel continued down the stairs and into a corridor brightly lit with long, fluorescent lights. Then there it was: At the end of the corridor, the figure was standing, facing her. No, it wasn't a figure. Isabel could see that it was a person. It was wearing some kind of an old-fashioned cloak. The person was small and stooped, his face covered by a hood.

He looked solid and real, and he was right in front of her. For a moment, Isabel just stared, not wanting to speak.

The figure spoke first: "Isabel." The voice was male and vaguely familiar.

"Yes," she said, keeping her voice firm only with effort.

"Isabel," the figure repeated, lifting its head. Slowly, he pulled away the hood, revealing a decayed face—gray and sick . . . rotting.

A scream escaped her lips as she stood, transfixed, by the horror in front of her.

Suddenly Isabel understood everything. She only hoped she had time to warn the others. Foolishly, she had walked into this, but they still had a chance. "Max!" she screamed as loudly as she could, turning to run.

Something grabbed her from behind. An invisible hand held her for a moment and then pulled her back away from the door and the stairs.

She tried to scream again, but found that her wind was gone. She heard the door slam, behind her. It was heavy and would drown out any further sounds she made.

"Isabel, you only just got here. I insist you stay a while," the voice behind her said.

13

The first scream jolted Kyle awake.

"Max!" he heard: The voice was dim, and sounded like it was coming from downstairs.

Isabel, his mind roared as he began climbing to his feet. He immediately saw that the door to her room was half open. He had a feeling that she was not inside, but he stepped through quickly to make sure. Seconds later, he had checked the bathroom and the walk-in closet. Nothing. That made sense—the scream sounded like it had come from far away.

From downstairs, he realized.

Kyle started moving. He had to get the others. Since no one else had come out of their rooms, he realized he had been the only one to hear her scream. The others couldn't hear through the heavy doors. His sleeping in the hallway had given Isabel a chance. He wouldn't blow it.

Running down the hallway, he stopped and banged his fists on Max and Liz's door, then on Michael and Maria's.

"It's Isabel! She's in trouble, I think she's downstairs!" he called out. Then he didn't wait another second. He took the stairs two at a time, thankful for his football training and his naturally good balance. He jumped the last five feet to the floor, calling, "Isabel!" at the top of his voice. For a moment he indulged in the hope that she had wandered downstairs to get something to eat and had gotten frightened. But she had screamed, and he knew Isabel wouldn't scream because she heard a noise or saw a cat. Something was wrong.

Kyle called out for her again. Though he was worried about Isabel, he felt the focus and concentration he had on the football field come to him. Even in the high-pressure games, Kyle had always kept his cool. Now, he was grateful for whatever his dad had passed on to him that let him keep his head.

He was trying to decide where to search first when he heard a squeak. He saw a doorway hanging slightly open near the pantry. Throwing the door open, he looked down an old staircase, into what he guessed was the basement.

He raced down the stairs, guessing that Isabel had come this way because the lights were on both in the basement and in the stairwell itself.

Maybe she just got locked in down there somewhere, he thought. Maybe they would be able to laugh about this in a few minutes, when he got her out. It was a possibility, but not a good one, because it didn't explain the scream.

Isabel would call out if she were trapped, but she had *screamed.*

His feet hit the basement floor, and he heard the door at the top of the stairs slam shut behind him. He ignored it.

"Isabel, are you here?" he called out, racing around the

basement, dodging furniture as he went.

"Kyle," he heard, but the sound was remote. Then he saw another open door with another well-lit staircase. He was sure that Isabel was down there. With any luck, she had just locked herself into a room in a sub-basement. He reminded himself to prop open any doors so the same thing didn't happen to him.

Kyle headed down the stairs and saw they were cut out of the bedrock. At the bottom of the stairs was a small landing, and a closed door. "Isabel?" he called out.

The reply was immediate and so clear that it surprised him. "Kyle, run! Stay away from him. Get the others and get out of here!"

She sounded scared, desperate. *It must be the Special Unit,* he thought. It was the only thing he could imagine evoking that kind of response from her.

"Noooo!" he heard Isabel scream, and he rushed for the door and yanked it open, surprised that it opened easily in his hand.

Game on, he thought as he raced into the room. Maybe he could rush whoever was there and catch them off guard. He saw two people at the end of the hallway. One was Isabel. She was just standing there. She looked scared, but unhurt. "Kyle, stop!" she yelled.

He came to a stop just a few steps away from Isabel and . . .

A thing.

No, he realized, it was a hunched-over . . . person, but there was something wrong—

"Kyle, get out," Isabel said, and her voice immediately drew his attention back to her. She was very still, as if she couldn't move.

"No, please stay," the thing said. Its voice was male, but it didn't look human. Correction: It looked like a human who had lived hard, and then died a while ago.

He took a step toward Isabel and said, "Come on, we're getting you out of here."

"You aren't going anywhere," the stranger said.

"Let him go, he has nothing to do with this," Isabel said.

"Step away from her, creep," he said, wondering how the figure could even be alive.

Then he realized that maybe it wasn't. Either way, he and Isabel were getting out of here now.

"Do not take another step," it said.

"Look, I don't like to pick on . . . whatever the hell you are, but you're scaring my friend here," Kyle said. He tensed his body, already planning his move. He would knock the thing down, then grab Isabel.

He bent his knees, pushed off with both feet, and tried to rush the creature only to find himself frozen in place.

"What the—?" he said.

"Like I said, you're not going anywhere," the creature said.

Something had grabbed Kyle's feet and was holding him to the floor.

I'm caught, his mind supplied. *Caught.*

There was a tightness in his chest. This thing was doing something to him. It had him, the same way it had Isabel.

"Isabel, I'm sorry," he said. He had blown it. He should have waited for Max or Michael. They would have been able to handle this better than him.

"Oh, Kyle," she said, fighting back tears and looking miserable due to her uncharacteristic helplessness.

"Kyle," the creature said, looking him over. There was something in its gaze that bothered Kyle, scared him more than the ruined and rotting flesh of its face. Was this a monster? A ghost?

He looked at Isabel, and it angered him to see her so scared. Whatever it was, what right did this thing have to do this to her? To *her* of all people? Kyle met the creature's gaze and when he spoke, he was surprised to hear his voice firm.

"I have to say, you don't look so good. I mean, you really look like hell," Kyle said. For a second, the creature seemed to be taken aback. Kyle continued, feeling his defiance rising. "I mean, you might really want to get that rash checked out."

Then the creature did something that surprised him. It smiled, with the side of its mouth that still had lips—the other was just teeth showing through ragged flesh.

"That was funny, Kyle. Go ahead and laugh, because I don't think you will find anything that happens from here on to be very funny," it said.

Max raced out into the hallway in bare feet. Michael was out an instant later.

"You heard it too?" Michael said.

Max nodded, and then he saw that Isabel's door was open. He was aware that Liz was behind him, but he was already racing down the hallway to his sister's room. He saw a pillow and blanket on the floor outside her door and ran inside with Michael behind him. They searched the room quickly.

When they came back out, Liz and Maria were waiting.

"No sign of Kyle or Isabel," Michael said.

Then Max noticed that Liz was holding out his sneakers, jeans, and a T-shirt. Maria was holding out Michael's clothes as well. Max realized he was only in his sleeping shorts. He quickly threw on the clothes, as Michael did the same.

"Something's wrong," Michael said. "Kyle said that something happened to Isabel. He must have gone after her."

"I think he was standing guard," Liz said, pointing to the pillow and blanket on the floor. Max nodded. That explained why they hadn't heard whatever happened to her, but Kyle did. He cursed himself for not following his instincts. They should have all stayed together tonight. Isabel had insisted on sleeping by herself, and now something had happened to her.

"You girls stay together, and Michael and I will—," Max began.

"No way," Maria said.

"Max, we can't," Liz said, her voice tight.

Max thought quickly—taking them would be dangerous. And so would leaving them. Better to stay together. And there was no time to argue.

"Michael and Maria, you head down these stairs," Max said, pointing to the rear stairs near Isabel's door. "We'll head down the front stairs and meet you in the middle. Call out if you see anything."

As they raced down the hallway, Max kept Liz in his peripheral vision. He saw that she had put on jeans and a T-shirt—one that he had never seen before. That was sensible, like bringing his shoes. They opened each of the bedroom doors and gave the rooms a quick scan. Nothing.

They hit the stairs, Max making sure that he was in the lead. He was especially wary because this was the place in Liz's vision where Maria had gone over the railing. But they made it down the stairs without incident and were in the front of the house. Keeping close together, they searched the front rooms. Then they moved to the center of the house, through the ballroom, and into the dining room, where Michael and Maria were waiting.

"Nothing," Michael reported.

Max nodded. They could not have gotten far. Kyle had been knocking at their door maybe three minutes ago. They could search the house more carefully, checking every closet and looking under every bed, but that would cost them precious time if Isabel and Kyle were outside. Still, they didn't have much choice.

"We'll start in the kitchen," Max said, realizing that he had fallen into his old habit of taking charge. Well, there was no time for long discussions and voting. Isabel might not have that time. For now, she'd be depending on him to do the right thing. *Like she depended on me once before,* Max thought. It had been another time on another world, and he had failed her then. He had failed her, and Michael, and himself.

He pushed those doubts out of his mind as they reached the kitchen. He looked around. Nothing was out of place. Then the door to the walk-in freezer caught his eye, and he raced over to it. Pulling it open, he looked inside. Nothing.

"Start trying doors," Max said.

He saw Liz open the pantry and head to the mini-hospital

they had found earlier. It was empty. He had just turned back when Michael called him over to the open door next to the pantry. Max could see the light from inside and immediately knew what he was looking at. Of course. How could he have missed it before, when they had first arrived and were searching the house?

Sloppy. Foolish and sloppy, he thought. And Isabel might pay for his mistake now. "Let's go," he said.

They all raced down the basement stairs. Before he could take another step, however, the light in the kitchen went out. Then the basement light went out as well. Max spun around and saw the light in the hallway go out as well. He grabbed Liz's hand. Then the rooms beyond went dark one by one.

A moment later, the light in the kitchen popped back on. Maria gave a startled cry, and Max could see Michael standing by the light switch.

"I don't like this," Michael said.

Max nodded. He didn't either.

Then there was a loud crashing sound from upstairs. Max felt Liz tense up, and then Maria let out a scream. The noise was followed by a loud banging sound that seemed to start from directly above them and travel toward the front of the house.

"Come on," Max said, already heading for the house's back stairs. This was the first definite sign of someone else being in the house. *Someone, or something,* he thought. Either way, Max decided he was ready; whoever was making that noise was no doubt involved with whatever had happened to Isabel and Kyle.

Racing up the stairs, Max immediately saw all doors

were closed, even though he and Liz had thrown all the doors open when they did their quick search on the way downstairs. Someone must have run through the hall, slamming the doors.

"Someone closed them," Max said, when the others had gathered next to him. Motioning his friends to stay back, he tried the first door, turning the knob and throwing it open. The room was empty.

He heard Michael and Maria try one across the hall. He grabbed Liz's hand again, and then went down the hall-way, opening doors as the other two did the same on their side. At the end, Max threw open Isabel's room, which was also empty.

"Someone's playing with us," Michael said, echoing Max's own thoughts.

"*Someone?*" Maria said.

"What?" Michael said.

"Do I have to spell it out? Do I have to be the only one who's willing to consider the obvious?" Maria said.

"You mean ghosts," Liz said.

"Well, big spooky house, missing people, loud noises. This is not brain surgery," Maria said.

"Maria—," Michael began.

"No, listen to me. Is it really any stranger than half-alien teenagers with cosmic powers?" she said.

Michael didn't look convinced, and neither did Max. There had to be a logical explanation.

"Whoever it is, it isn't the Special Unit," Liz said.

"Whoever it is, we need to find them, and find Isabel and Kyle," Michael said.

"And what about Liz's vision?" Maria asked.

"We are not defenseless," Michael said, confidence in his voice.

"Well, neither was Isabel, but—," Maria said.

Before Michael could respond, Max raised his hand and said, "We need to be very careful. Whatever or whoever it is, we'll deal with it. The most important thing now is to find Isabel and Kyle . . ." *Before it's too late,* he finished silently. He saw that he didn't have to say it. Everyone was thinking the same thing.

"Maria is right about one thing," Michael said. "Something got Isabel, in spite of her powers."

"They may have caught her by surprise, and there are more of us," Max added. "Whatever happens, we have to stay together, or at least in pairs. No one goes anywhere alone."

A loud crash downstairs broke his train of thought. "Michael, you and Maria—" Max hesitated for a moment, remembering Liz's vision. They needed to keep Maria away from the top of the front stairs. "You take the back stairs, Liz and I will take the front," Max said. He would have rather kept the four of them together, but they had come up that way and had given whoever it was a chance to disappear down the opposite staircase.

There was more noise downstairs, and when Max and Liz hit the great room, they saw furniture lying everywhere. Someone had turned over chairs and tables, and had done it quickly.

"Max, look," Liz said.

He turned to see a blazing fire in the fireplace, where moments ago the fire was almost out. "Michael!" he called out.

"No one here!" came the muffled reply from the other end of the house.

"Wait there!" Max said, heading back through the house. There was some more overturned furniture in the dining room. Michael and Maria were waiting at the bottom of the back stairs, just outside the kitchen.

"Whoever it is, they're gone," Michael said. "What now?"

There was something bugging Max. There was one part of the house they hadn't checked. "Back to the kitchen," he ordered.

A few seconds later, they were in the kitchen, and Max sensed that something was wrong. "Max, look," Liz said, pointing to the plastic that had covered the back door to the house. Someone had re-sealed it. No, more than that: It looked like it had never been torn. It was odd. *If someone, or something, is trying to scare us, why bother with the plastic?* Max wondered.

There was another loud crash, this time from below them, followed by a loud banging sound.

"The basement," Max said, spying the open door near the pantry. He couldn't remember whether they had shut it before, but it didn't matter—he had the feeling that the answer was down there. "Come on," he said, taking the lead.

Before he took the first step, he felt a hand on his shoulder. "Wait a minute, Max, I don't like this," Michael said.

Max thought about it for a moment. Something did feel wrong here, but Isabel was in trouble. He turned to Michael and said, "Neither do I."

Then he started down the stairs.

14

The basement was so full of junk that Max couldn't tell if anything had been disturbed, but this had been the source of the noise. And who or whatever had been making a racket in the house, had come down here—he was nearly sure of that.

"Let's all stay together," Max said, leading the group around the basement. Old bicycles, furniture, a boiler . . . but no Isabel and no Kyle. "I think we've been led down here," he said.

"I think you're right, Max," Liz said.

"I have the same feeling, but why lead us around?" Michael said.

"That's what ghosts do, they try to scare you," Maria said.

"Okay, let's say it's a ghost—a big, mean, nasty ghost. Why the wild goose chase? Why not just strike us down with its ghostly powers?" Michael asked.

"A trap," Liz said.

"Or it's trying to separate us," Maria said.

"Why bother, if the ghost is powerful enough to take on Isabel and Kyle? Why does it care if we get separated?" Michael said.

"Because people are more scared when they're alone," Maria said.

Max nodded. There was something to that. Had the person they were after been leading them in different directions to try to pick them off one at a time? "It makes sense," Max said. "As far as we know, Isabel and Kyle were both alone when they disappeared."

"Ghosts, Max?" Michael said, raising his eyebrows in disbelief.

"I think Maria is onto something. We need to stay together," Max said. Then he spotted another partly open door, hanging in toward the basement. "There," he said, pointing.

"If you guys are right, that door could be leading us into a trap," Michael said.

"Maybe, but even if it is a trap, it's the only lead we have to Isabel and Kyle and whoever might have them," Max said.

"It seems like this *ghost* is staying one step ahead of us," Michael said.

"Then we'll have to be very careful," Max responded, throwing the door open. It led to another staircase that led up to steel doors. "I think it goes outside," he said.

"Max, let me go first," Michael said, trying to push forward.

"No," Max said, holding back his friend with one hand. "Stay behind Liz and Maria." When he got to the top of the stairs, he pushed against the double steel doors. At first they didn't budge and he pushed again, this time with his shoulder, prepared to use his powers if they didn't give. But the doors swung open once he applied some pressure and Max's momentum carried him several steps outside. He barely kept to his feet on the muddy ground.

"Max!" he heard Michael shout.

Then his friends were next to him.

"You were saying about being careful?" Michael said.

Max looked around. They were in the rear of the house, near the garage, where they had parked the van. The steel doors must have been for deliveries, maybe even for coal when the house was built.

"At least it stopped raining," Liz noticed.

Max saw that she was right. In fact, the night had gotten pretty clear. There were still clouds in the sky, but he could see stars, and the nearly full moon gave them enough light to see.

Scanning the grounds, Max took in the large pool, which was empty except for a few feet of dirty water. There was a tennis court, a field, and the remains of a garden with a large fountain in the center.

Once again, he couldn't shake the feeling that someone was playing with them. And whoever he was, he had Isabel and Kyle. Too much time had passed already; he had to do something *now*. He had to act before it was too late for Isabel.

Something flashed behind the fountain. Max knew instinctively that this was it. Then he was moving, with Michael and Maria on his left and Liz on his right.

"What was it?" Michael asked.

"I saw someone in the garden. We're going to stop this

right now," he said. He told himself this would turn out all right. He would make it all right. He would not fail Isabel again, not in this life.

Max and the others reached the fountain and saw what looked like a hooded and caped figure disappear behind an overgrown bush. Angling around it, Max couldn't see anything but a jumble of weeds and plants he couldn't identify.

"There," Michael called, pointing to movement in a hedge maybe a hundred yards ahead. Max nodded, and the group headed in that direction. They had to dodge a maze of plants, and more than once, Max felt something scratch his arms.

They reached the hedge, which, Max realized, marked the outer barrier of the garden. There were no breaks in the hedge, and they wouldn't be able to get through it easily. The growth was thick, and the hedge was nearly three times his height. *Maybe the person we're chasing knows a hidden passage through it,* he thought. *Or maybe it can just walk through solid objects.*

Maybe Maria was right. Were they dealing with a ghost? Or a spirit? Was that idea any stranger than his own existence as an alien-human hybrid? If this was a spirit, Max sensed it was evil. Was it more powerful than them? It probably had Isabel and Kyle, so it wasn't powerless. On the other hand, it had not tried to take them all at once, so there might be some limit to its powers.

Max waved his hand and two sections of the hedge parted, making enough room for them to pass through two at a time. On the other side of the hedge, they stared out at an open field maybe two hundred yards across and ending at the bottom of a tree-covered hill.

The hooded figure was about halfway across the field when Max caught sight of him. He and the others immediately started after it. "Liz, is that who or what you saw in your vision?" Max asked.

"I think it might be," Liz responded.

"Michael, stay with Liz and Maria," Max said, racing into the lead.

He could hear Michael's complaints, but he would not let the thing they were chasing get away. Not when Isabel's life might depend on him ending this now. Max was quickly closing the gap between them. Max was less than fifty yards behind whatever it was when the figure stepped into the trees at the bottom of the hill. From that point on, Max had a difficult time tracking the figure in the trees and heavy brush. A few seconds later, Max was at the tree line himself. He felt a hand on his shoulder and spun around to see Michael staring at him. "We agreed to stay together," Michael said.

"You're right," Max said, as Liz and Maria caught up. Together, the group headed up the hill.

"You're not getting into the spirit of this democracy thing," Michael said.

"Sorry," Max said. "I thought I could get him."

"We'll *all* get him," Liz said.

Max nodded. They were stronger together. "Anyone see anything?" he asked.

No one responded, but as they got closer to the top of the hill, Michael said, "I see him."

At the top, the figure stood still for a minute and stared down at them.

"Hey! Stop!" Michael said. For a moment, the figure seemed to be listening. It remained still, watching them. Then it disappeared from view behind the top of the hill.

Max kept himself super alert, watching for any signs of the figure. Michael turned to Max. "This feels like a trap, Maxwell." Max nodded. He felt the same thing. They had been playing the figure's game up until now. He or it had led them through the house and out here.

"Should we just walk into it, then?" Michael said.

"Yes," Max said, keeping his voice low. "He'll think he has us, but we have a few surprises of our own." Max wondered if Isabel had even had a chance to use her powers on the figure.

"Do you think our powers will even work on ghosts?" Michael asked.

"If it really is a ghost, we'll find out," Max said.

"The way I feel, I wouldn't want to be that ghost right now," Michael said.

"I know what—," Max began.

"What are you guys talking about?" Maria asked, leaning forward.

Michael turned to her and said, "Advanced military strategy, nothing for you to worry your pretty little head about."

There was a loud smack, and Max didn't have to turn around to know what caused it.

"Kidding," Michael said, raising his hands.

When they were near the top of the hill, Max stopped the group and said, "Let Michael and me get a few paces ahead."

"Wait," Maria said.

"We're better able to deal with a threat," Max said.

"You know, alien powers and all that," Michael added.

"Liz, you and Maria will have our backs," Max added. Liz nodded, and he knew she understood.

"Okay, we'll check out the top, make sure he doesn't get by us," Max said.

The girls nodded as Max and Michael took the last few steps. Leaning down, they peered over the top of the hill, which was actually a peak of some sort. The hill on the other side looked steep.

"Careful, we don't know how far down it is," Max warned.

"Max?" Liz whispered from behind them.

"Nothing yet," Max said, getting up slowly as Michael did the same. He took a few steps forward, scanning the area for any sign of the figure. He took a few steps down the other side of the hill, when he felt Michael grab his arm. Then Michael pointed down the hill with one hand while he grabbed a tree with the other hand.

Max immediately saw what Michael was pointing to. This side of the hill was much steeper, more of a cliff than a hill, leading down to a good-sized stream at least a hundred yards down.

"What is it?" Maria said from behind them.

"Don't come up here, it's very steep," Michael said.

"Yes, it's very dangerous," a voice said from Max's right.

His head immediately pivoted to see the figure they had been chasing standing less than twenty yards from them. In the dim light, Max couldn't make out any of its features, especially with the hood partly covering his face. But it was a he—Max could tell that much from his voice.

"We want our friends, right now," Max said, his voice firm.

"Max?" Liz called, as the girls came close enough to see the figure. Max waved his hand and they stopped, just on the other side of the hill's peak.

Then the figure took a few steps toward Max and Michael.

"We don't want any trouble," Max said. "We just want to take our friends and go."

"You shouldn't have come," the figure said.

"In a minute you're going to wish we hadn't," Michael said. He was about to explode, Max realized. They couldn't afford that now, not until they had Isabel and Kyle safe. After that, all bets would be off.

The figure laughed, the sound high-pitched and unpleasant. Then it began to cough. When it was finished, it pulled back its hood to reveal its ruined face.

He's sick, Max thought. *No, not sick, it looks like he's . . . dead.* With his peripheral vision, Max saw Michael jump slightly at the sight and heard both Liz and Maria gasp. He felt a crawling revulsion himself. Was this person dead? Was he seeing a ghost? Or something worse?

"Hey, freak show," Michael said. "How about you tell us where our friends are and we don't hurt you." The creature just stared at them. "We're not impressed by your tricks or your scary mask. We're not afraid of you," Michael continued, taking a step forward and raising his right hand.

The creature was silent for a moment and seemed to be sizing them up. "Too bad," it finally said. "You should be."

The creature raised its own hand, and Max felt something grab him, something he couldn't see. Then he was stumbling forward, down the side of the hill. He heard Liz scream, and then he was flying through space.

Liz felt something touch her and shove her backward. Her arms went pinwheeling behind her, and she knew she was going down. Then Liz hit the ground and rolled to a stop, her face pressing down in the wet leaves and mud. Turning her head, she saw Maria close by in the same position.

"Maria," she said. Her friend immediately turned in her direction and nodded. She seemed okay. "Michael!" she cried, starting to get up. Then something caught Maria's eye, and she looked forward and screamed. Liz pivoted her head and saw the creature heading toward them.

Liz thought that whatever it was, it looked too real to be a ghost—but it didn't look alive, either, since its gray flesh was literally falling off its face and hands. The hood and cape just made it look creepier. About five paces away, the creature stood, looming over them.

"What did you do to Michael?" Maria said. Liz was surprised to hear anger in her voice, not fear. Liz felt the same thing. She saw Maria starting to get up, and did the same.

"Don't worry, you will be joining him soon," the figure said.

There was a flash of movement, and a rock hit the creature on the forehead with a thud, then dropped to the ground. It was immediately followed by a good-sized piece of the creature's forehead.

The creature howled, and its hand immediately went to its head. Liz grabbed for a stick, took two steps forward, and swung at the creature. It turned at the last instant and tried to duck, but it was too late.

The stick struck it in the side of the head, bouncing up

and off the skull and—Liz noted—taking a chunk of hair and scalp with it. The creature fell onto its back and gave another howl of surprise and fear. Liz didn't hesitate; she turned and grabbed Maria's hand. "Come on," she said, pulling her friend away from the creature and toward the house.

"What about Michael and Max?" Maria said, resisting.

"I think they're okay," Liz said. She was nearly sure of it. Once before, when Max had died, she had felt that event as certainly as she would had it happened to her. Now, she thought Max was all right. He was probably hurt after his tumble down the hill, but he was alive.

She saw the dazed figure behind them start to struggle to get up. "Come on, we need to lead it away from the guys."

They ran down the hill. Liz turned around only once to make sure the creature was behind them. He was, and she was glad to see that he was moving slowly. They had hurt him.

What kind of ghost gets hurt when you hit him in the head? Liz wondered. It didn't make sense, but there was no time to think about it. She and Maria were on the open ground and sprinting for the house. She didn't have a plan, except to give Max and Michael time to get their bearings. If they were hurt, Max could heal them. Then they could come and deal with the creature and find Isabel and Kyle.

As they reached the back of the house, Liz spared another glance behind her. The creature was following, more quickly than before. They had less than half a minute's lead now. Liz considered heading around the house and leading the creature away entirely, but she didn't like the way he was gaining. She felt their best chance lay inside. There, they could move around and try to hide in one of the mansion's many rooms. The creature would waste valuable time looking for them—time that Max and Michael could use.

So when she hit the back door, she flung it open and pulled Maria inside. Then she turned an ancient deadbolt to lock the door, and the two girls headed for the kitchen. They stopped for a moment to catch their breath, and Liz realized the house was deathly quiet.

"What's the plan?" Maria asked. Her friend was scared, but Maria was keeping it together. She had come a long way since the day Liz had first told her the truth about Max, Isabel, and Michael. That made sense, because Liz had come a long way too.

"We stay away from him," Liz said.

"What, like hide?" Maria said.

"We need to buy the guys time," Liz said.

Liz could see fear on her friend's face, but this wasn't fear for herself—it was for Michael. And this fear didn't make Maria weaker, it made her stronger. Liz could see that in Maria's eyes, along with the worry.

"I really think they're okay," Liz said, praying she was right. "Come on, we'll hide upstairs. It's too open down here. We only have to give the guys a few minutes. If that thing searches the house for us, it will take a while. And if he comes upstairs, we'll run down the opposite stairway."

"You call that a plan? Run and hide?" Maria said.

"Best I could do on short notice," Liz said.

"Okay, but this way, I want to get something." Liz nodded and followed Maria through the house. When they reached the fireplace, Maria went to the small rack nearby and picked up an iron poker. She handed it to Liz. Then she took one for herself.

Maria smiled and said, "So we can give Frankenstein another surprise."

Liz nodded again as Maria headed toward the curving front stairs. Images from her vision sprang to her mind. She considered heading through the house and taking the back stairs, then she dismissed the idea. For one, it would take more time. Secondly, in the vision, Maria had been running from the other direction. For now, the front stairs were safest.

Maria led the way up the stairs, holding the metal poker firmly in one hand. The girls moved quickly, trying to make as little noise as possible.

As they neared the top, Liz was unnerved by the fact that they could not hear any more noise. *It is somewhere in the house,* Liz thought. And it knew the house very well, much better than they did.

The second they stepped on the landing, Liz heard a crash downstairs. The sound came from the bottom of the stairs, somewhere in the living room. Without a word, Liz and Maria sprinted down the hallway. *He knows we're up here,* Liz thought. The house wasn't safe now. Maybe they could make it down the back stairs and then outside again. There were plenty of woods out there.

They crossed the hallway in seconds and started to slow down when they reached the other side, preparing to head down the stairs. Liz was in front, and they were about ten feet from the end when the creature came up the stairs.

The girls stopped dead, and Liz had to stifle a scream when she saw it with its hood off in the light of the hallway. *How can anything that looks like that still be alive?* she thought.

Maybe it isn't, her brain answered.

Maria took a few steps forward and raised her poker. "This is for my boyfriend," she said, bringing it down hard.

Watching her, Liz raised her own and got ready to swing it, but it got stuck in the air. Liz saw that Maria seemed frozen in space.

"Don't worry about your boyfriend," the creature said in a gravelly voice. "I would worry more about yourselves."

Suddenly, the poker in Liz's hand got too hot to hold. She let go at the same moment Maria did. Both pieces of iron hung in the air for a moment, then shot across the hallway, imbedding themselves into the wall.

Liz heard screaming and realized that one of the screams was hers. She didn't wait to see what happened next. Simultaneously, she and Maria turned around and ran.

Time seemed to slow like it did in a dream . . . or a vision. Then Liz realized why this moment seemed familiar: It was her vision. Maria was slightly ahead of her and sprinting down the hallway with a monster behind her.

Liz wanted to scream for Maria to stop, but then what? There was a monster behind them. And Liz had no illusions: This monster was deadly. Their only chance was to keep going, to get away. But she had seen that in her vision, and she knew how that dream ended for Maria.

Liz ran for her life.

15

In her slowed dreamtime, Liz wished for powers like Max's. He would be able to fight that thing, whatever it was. Liz had powers of her own, but now they seemed like a cruel joke: They would merely allow her to see her best friend die twice. She could also sometimes move objects with her mind and release energy as well, but she couldn't do either on demand. And she had almost no control.

There has to be another way, she thought, looking behind her. The creature was close behind them. The problem was that the balcony was just ahead of them and then it was at least thirty feet to the floor.

For a moment, she wanted to grab Maria so they could turn and fight. It was what Max would do, even if he knew the fight was lost from the beginning. Liz might have done it, too, except Maria was going too fast and was too close to the balcony for Liz to stop her now. She was going to go over, and Liz was going to watch her. . . .

For the second time.

Liz felt a moment of helplessness, and then realized

that, while she didn't have Max's powers, it didn't mean she was powerless. And she didn't have to *stop* Maria. Of course, there was only one chance, and even if she succeeded in what she wanted to do, there was no guarantee that she or Maria would survive. Well, there were never any guarantees. She had learned that three years ago when she was shot at the Crashdown. A miracle had brought her back, and since then she had been living on borrowed time.

Liz Parker saw her one chance and took it. They were just a few feet from the edge. The only thing that pushed Liz to take action was that, in this instant, she was more afraid for Maria than she was of anything else.

Reaching out with both hands, she grabbed at the back of Maria's jeans, getting a tight grip on the denim. Then Liz took one step to the left and pulled with all of her might as she threw all of her weight to the left. The result was just what Liz was hoping for: They were still moving forward, but angling to the left. A fraction of a second later, Liz saw that Maria was going to miss the railing.

Instead, both girls were barreling toward the large, curving staircase. Liz felt a momentary rush of satisfaction. She had prevented her vision from coming true. Maria did not go over the balcony. But she and Liz were now racing over the edge of the staircase. Then they hurtled over the edge, and Liz felt her feet leave the floor.

She had a single clear thought as she and Maria launched themselves into space: *It's a long way down.*

Max woke up slowly. The closer he came to consciousness, the more he felt the pain in his head. For a moment, he considered allowing himself to slip back into darkness. At least, it hadn't hurt so much when he was there.

No, there's something I have to do, he thought.

Then it all came flooding back: the house. Isabel gone. The creature at the top of the hill. There was danger to his friends . . . to Liz.

Max tried to push himself up and found that his body was not cooperating. He sent the commands to his arms, but they moved sluggishly and didn't push him hard enough to sit up—let alone get up.

He took an inventory of his pains and realized there were cuts and scrapes and a significant pain in his left shoulder, but the worst, by far, was the pain in his head. Slowly, he reached back with his hand and felt for the back of his head. When his fingers finally got there, they found his hair matted and wet. No, not wet, slick.

He was bleeding pretty heavily. He knew a blow to the back of the head could be serious and that there might be a concussion. He needed to take care of that before he did anything else, but his mind was slow, mushy.

Not a good sign, he thought. But his friends were depending on him. . . .

Michael, he thought. Michael had fallen with him. Max tried to lift his head to look for his friend, or to call out, but his physical responses were off.

Definitely not good, he thought.

He would have to heal his himself first, at least his head. It was hard to concentrate, but he forced himself. Max kept his hand on the split in his scalp.

Summoning his powers and reaching out with his mind, he saw the split in the skin. That would be easy to repair. But there was something else: His skull was cracked as well.

Focusing his energy, he willed the bone to heal. Then he brought the skin together, keeping his hand there to eliminate the swelling and any other damage in the area. After a few seconds, his head cleared and it was like waking suddenly from a deep sleep.

Max was alert, which made him even more conscious of the pain coming from half a dozen places on his body. He brushed them aside and got to his feet. His right knee protested slightly, but it held.

"Michael!" he called out, but there was no response. Looking around, he saw a tree behind him, which had a dent in the bark and a dark spot. That must have been where he'd hit his head. Looking up, he saw that he was maybe thirty yards from the top of the hill. He could see the path he had taken down when the creature had . . . what? What had the creature done to him and Michael? It had pushed them off the top, but it had never physically touched either of them. Did this thing have powers like his? Well, Max wouldn't be caught by surprise twice.

A few feet to his right, he saw what must have been Michael's path down the hill. There were broken saplings and flattened brush. Michael had come to a rest just above Max, maybe ten yards closer to the top. Max found the spot at the end of the trail. There was some blood there, but no Michael.

Just when Max thought Michael had gotten back up the hill on his own, he saw another path through the brush. This one was smoother and more regular. Suddenly, Max was sure that the creature had come back and dragged

Michael to the house while Max lay unconscious.

But why? And why leave Max? Too many questions and no time to answer them. Max started up the hill and felt his knee twitch. He ignored it, as he ignored the other cuts and scrapes—except the one on his left shoulder. That one was bad and made it hard to move his arm. He knew that soon he would have to fight. He couldn't afford the handicap, so he used his good hand and covered the area.

As he walked, he reached out with his powers. There was a deep puncture in his left shoulder that probably was from a broken branch. It healed quickly, which was a pleasant surprise. In the past, he had found that it was harder to heal himself than to heal others. And it usually required greater concentration.

A year ago he would not have been able to manage it that easily. His powers were growing, developing. And right now, that meant only one thing to him: He would be in a better position to save his friends.

It's my fault it has them, he thought. He had insisted they come here to hide from the Special Unit. He had allowed Isabel to sleep in her own room. And he had agreed to separate rooms for the rest of them because he had wanted to be alone with Liz.

He had failed his sister and Michael, for the second time. Just like he had failed them and everyone else on their home planet. And he had failed Liz and Maria and Kyle, who depended on him to make the right decisions, whether or not he wanted the job of leader. Well, he might not be fit to be king, but he was fit to fight this creature, to make up for some part of his failures.

He was up over the top of the hill and down the side

quickly. By the time he was in the open field, the pain in his body had receded from his consciousness. All he could think about was Liz and his friends in the hands of that . . . thing. Well, ghost or not, the creature was going to regret messing with them tonight.

He ran across the field, looking up at the moon, which was now much lower in the sky. He must have been out for a couple of hours at least. Plenty of time for *anything* to happen to his friends. Max pushed the thought aside. It wouldn't help them, and he needed to focus on what he had to do. And he had to do it coldly, without getting lost in his feelings.

His knee throbbed at the stress of his sprint across the field, but he ignored it. There was no time to heal it now. When he reached the house, he was not surprised to see the metal basement doors open. The light was on inside. He headed down the basement stairs quickly and came to another open door and another staircase.

Max knew his friends and that thing that had taken them were down those stairs. He also knew that this was some sort of trap. Well, the creature may have thought it had him, and it *had* caught him by surprise on the hill, but there were some things it didn't know about him—things that Max would show it soon.

Max bounded down the stairs, careful of his injured knee, and stepped through a door that revealed a short corridor brightly lit with strong fluorescent light. At the end of the corridor was another heavy door, which he reached in seconds. As he opened the door, he felt ready for anything as he stepped into the next room. The creature was standing at the end of a large room, waiting for him. Max lifted his hand, ready to blast the thing with everything he had when he took in the rest of the room. For a moment, he was too stunned to move.

"Get out of here!" Liz screamed.

"Run!" Isabel said.

Max didn't move. He looked at his sister and his friends. They were each restrained somehow in open semicircular glass chambers on each wall. Isabel, Liz, and Maria were on one side, Kyle and Michael on the other. There were at least a dozen empty chambers on each side as well, all closed. There were computers and pieces of household electronics that Max recognized. And there was other equipment that Max had never seen before. The combination of the two made the place look thrown together. For an insane moment, he had the feeling that he was looking at Dr. Frankenstein's laboratory.

"Go ahead and blast me," the creature said, "but if you do, your friends will die."

Max felt his head swim. There was something going on here that was stranger than ghosts and evil spirits. He shook off his doubts. Whatever the thing in front of him was, it was real, and that meant it could be hurt—or killed. Max got the feeling that that wouldn't be hard to do. The creature was literally falling apart. And its labored breathing and croaking voice told Max that the thing would die soon, whether or not Max did anything to it.

"Maxwell, get out of here," Michael said. Max resisted the temptation to look at his friend. From his voice, Max could tell that Michael was in pain. His peripheral vision told him that Liz and the others were alive. That would have to be enough for now. He kept his eyes on the creature and demanded, "Who are you and what is this place?"

The creature gave a short laugh and said, "You haven't figured it out yet, Max? I'm not surprised; you never were very quick. . . ."

The thing looked at him, and Max recognized something in its eyes, despite the ruined gray flesh around them.

". . . Zan."

A flood of realization hit Max. It couldn't be. It made perfect sense, but it was plainly impossible.

"Oh, my God!" Isabel cried.

16

"It can't be you," Isabel said. For a moment, she couldn't say the name. When she finally did, she spat it out: "*Nicholas.*"

"In the flesh, as it were," he said. Then he stepped closer to Isabel and smiled—at least the one side of his face that still had lips curled upward. "After all we've been through, I'm glad to see you recognize me."

Isabel couldn't believe it, but it *was* Nicholas: She could see the shadows of him in his ruined face and in his voice. "You should be dead by now," she said.

"I really should be," Nicholas said. "All the others are dead, thanks to you all. And this husk is way past its expiration date."

"Isabel, you know this guy?" Kyle asked.

"We all do," Isabel replied. "He was one of the Skins in Copper Summit."

"Not just one of them, my dear. I am Kevar's voice on this planet," Nicholas said. "You should show some respect. Kevar is your king."

"Just kill him, Max, and let's get out of here," Michael said.

To Isabel's surprise, Max raised his hand and seemed like he was about to do just that.

"Don't do it, Max," Nicholas said, raising one hand in the air. He was hiding a small remote control of some kind.

"If I die, your friends die," Nicholas said.

"He's bluffing," Michael said. "Do it."

"This controls the electrodes that are attached to your friends' heads," he said, then he thumbed the control and Isabel felt her head turn to fire. She could hear Michael call out as well.

"Okay, stop!" Max said, but he didn't put his hand down.

"See the electrodes on each of their foreheads? They are directly over the cerebral cortex. A mild charge disrupts your special abilities. That's a little trick I learned from your friends in the Special Unit. They know quite a bit about your physiology. Too bad you didn't stay long enough for them to do a proper dissection," Nicholas said.

"You're working with the Special Unit," Isabel said.

"We don't exactly work together, but they've been useful," Nicholas replied.

"You were the one who told them where we were," Max said.

"An anonymous tip," he said. "Like I said, they have been useful. Actually, I had wanted them to save me the trouble of capturing you, but you didn't cooperate."

Isabel felt the beginnings of an idea and decided to keep him talking. He was vain—a braggart, actually.

Maybe he would reveal something they could use.

"How did you find us?" Isabel asked.

"A happy accident. You wandered into the range of my equipment. Really lucky for me. I'm not feeling so well these days. I don't know if I would have had time to grow another husk," Nicholas said.

"You did something to our van?" Isabel said. Suddenly things were becoming clear to her, and she felt a rising anger.

"You were painfully easy to manipulate. When you escaped the Special Unit, a little bright light to attract you to this spot and a little car trouble, and you wandered right into my hands. You humans, even half-humans, are a depressingly simple species," Nicholas said.

"You set it all up. The Bentons? The book? Everything?" she said.

"Actually, my dear, there really was a family called the Bentons, and a crazy old man who raved through these halls for years. Fortunately, he kept this remote house in good condition. Perfect for me to grow some new friends," he said.

The Bentons had lived and died in this house. But how much of what she had felt had been real? She couldn't believe that he had come here, disturbed this house that had been such a good place—a comfortable place. He had brought his evil here, his rotting stink, sullying whatever the Bentons had left of themselves in this house. She wasn't just angry now, she was furious. "That was you calling my name?" Isabel said.

"And you came so quickly. Investigating ghosts, Vilandra? You were always flighty, but I think you have let these simple, superstitious humans get to you," Nicholas mocked.

"That's what the plastic is for," Liz said. "And the food. More of the husks."

Nicholas looked at Liz with approval. "Max, it looks like your taste in women is improving."

"Stay away from her!" Max said, his voice booming.

To Isabel's surprise, Nicholas took a step back. *He's afraid. He doesn't want to die,* she thought.

"You're right. New husks need a clean environment," Nicholas said, then he turned back to Isabel. "I'm growing a special one for myself, something I think you will like. Tall and strapping. Perfect for your shallow sensibilities."

He stared at her as if he knew something about her. In the past, he had claimed that she and he were lovers on their home world. But he had also claimed that she had betrayed her brother and her people, and she had learned that was a lie. "Kill him, Max," she found herself saying.

Nicholas turned quickly to face Max. "I wouldn't, Max. This device has what you might call a dead man's switch. If I let go of it, your friends will get the shock of their lives," he said, flashing his rotting grin. "Now, with your abilities, you might be able to heal them, save one, maybe two, before it's too late. But which ones?"

Isabel saw the pain on Max's face. There had to be something she could do to help. She tried to summon her powers, but found Nicholas had been telling the truth about them being blocked. And with her hands strapped behind her and attached somehow to the chamber, she could hardly move. Still, there had to be something. . . .

Then there was the beginnings of an idea.

Isabel remembered seeing similar chambers in Copper Summit. The ones holding her and her friends looked different, more crude, but similar. She remembered the day in Copper Summit when she had seen them, when she had first met Nicholas.

"What's your plan? I don't think you're going to last until the new husks are grown. Doesn't that take twenty years?" Isabel asked.

"True"—he nodded—"but I've improved the process. Necessity is a mother, you know. And I don't mind saying that it was tricky with this planet's limited technology. You destroyed all of our best equipment back in Copper Summit. It was like using stone knives and bearskins to create a growth chamber. . . . Still, I did it." Nicholas leaned into her. "Impressed, dear?"

Isabel spat in his ruined face. "You had fifty years to get us the first time. Do you really think another fifty will make a difference?" she said.

"Well, it looks like I won't even need that long," Nicholas said. "It looks like my mission is almost complete."

"Your mission?" she asked.

"Bring the Granilith back to Kevar, and with it, the head of Zan," Nicholas said.

"Well, it looks like you're going to have to go home empty-handed," Michael said, "because you'll get nothing from us."

"Really?" Nicholas said, and then he turned to Max. "You wouldn't sacrifice yourself for your friends? Give me a little artifact to save your sister, your friends and your new mate? Gotten a little coldhearted over the years, have we, Zan?"

"Don't listen to him, Max. You can't trust him," Michael said.

Isabel could see the pain on Max's face. He would sacrifice himself for her, or for any of them, but she couldn't allow it.

"You think that if you do that, you'll return to Kevar a hero?" Isabel challenged.

"Mission accomplished, and for that I get one of the five worlds to control," he said.

Isabel nodded. "I'm sure Kevar values your services, but why didn't he recall you home before you fell apart?"

"This isn't the movies, Isabel. Space travel is not that simple," he said.

"Really? Kevar didn't mention that when he was here," she said.

"What?" Nicholas said. "Kevar was never here."

"Of course he was. He came to get me, said there was new technology for the return trip. He said I could go home," Isabel said.

Nicholas looked stricken, then furious. "You're lying!" he screamed. "This is a trick."

"He wanted me to come with him," Isabel said. "Odd that he would offer me a trip home just to get me in the sack, but not to you—his valued aid—when your life depended on it."

Doubt flashed across Nicholas's face.

"It's true, you know it is," Isabel said.

"Yeah, that's the problem with backstabbing weasels like Kevar. You just can't trust them," Michael said.

Nicholas was quiet for a long moment, then he raised his head and leveled his gaze at Isabel. "Kevar's a born leader. He does what he has to do," he said.

"You just keep telling yourself that," Isabel replied. "For all you know, he has no more use for you. If he even allows you to come home, you don't know what you'll find. Or what kind of welcome you'll get."

Nicholas only shrugged. "I know what happens if I stay here. I'm stuck on this backwater excuse for a planet forever. No thanks. I'll take my chances with our glorious leader." He spun around and said to Max, "It will be worth it to see his expression when I throw your head at his feet."

Isabel saw a twisted smile on his face and a wild look in his eyes. *More than his body is falling apart,* she thought. *He's losing it.* But he still had a cunning intelligence that Isabel didn't like.

He turned to Max. "It's time to stop playing games."

"Let them go, or I will kill you—right here, right now," Max said. There was steel in his voice.

Nicholas laughed, a grating sound from a decaying throat. "And watch your friends die? I know you too well. You never could make sacrifices. That's why you're here and Kevar is sitting on your throne. History repeats itself, Max. Destiny brought you here. Do you believe in destiny, Max? I do. I've always been a student of history—even Earth history, stupid and short as it is. And there is one thing that I've learned: There are always patterns and cycles. History does repeat itself, Max. You're here so I can defeat you again, so I can kill you again, just like I did last time. That should suit you, Max. You die, but you save your friends. It's so predictable, it's so you. A martyr's death, but this time, no one but us will know or care. Of course, if you choose to fight, you will probably beat me. My powers aren't what they used to be," Nicholas taunted.

"Don't do it, Max," Liz called out. "End this now. If you give him what he wants, he'll kill us all, anyway."

Max looked from Liz to Nicholas, then to the rest of his friends. "You'll let them go if I go with you?" Max said.

"No Max!" Michael said.

"*And* show me where the Granilith is," Nicholas said. "Do that and they will all be free to live out their lives on this puny rock."

"Max, don't," Liz pleaded, tears running down her face.

Max looked at her for a moment, and then he lowered his hand. "Okay, how do you want to do this?" he said.

"First, I need you to do something for me. You see, I've been feeling a little under the weather lately. You need to fix that, or this husk won't last long enough to do what we have to do," Nicholas said.

"I don't know if I can," Max said.

"You'll have to, if you want to save your friends. That's the deal," Nicholas stated.

"What guarantee do I have that you'll keep your end of the bargain?" Max asked.

"Well, I can guarantee that if you don't do as I say, your friends will die," he said. Then he lowered his voice. "Once I have you and the Granilith, I don't need them. Kevar doesn't need them. I'm prepared to leave the non-combatants out of this, but it's up to you."

Max was quiet for a long time, then he nodded and said, "I'll do it."

17

Max felt defeated. *I've failed them again,* he thought, looking at Isabel and Michael. He had led them to destruction before, now he had done it again. And this time he'd led Liz there, too, along with Kyle and Maria.

They had all depended on him, whether he had wanted the job or not. Now they were in the hands of an alien who had had one purpose for the last fifty years: to find him. Well, Nicholas could have him. His life was worth Liz's, or Isabel's or any of his friends.

At least then his life would mean something, something more than it had had up until now. It seemed like he had done nothing in his eighteen years but protect his secret, protect himself. Was that why he had come here? Was that why he had been re-created and sent halfway across the galaxy, to protect himself while others made the sacrifices that counted? Liz had sacrificed too much for him. Alex had sacrificed his life. Isabel had given up any chance at a normal life of her own.

Well, that would all change now. He didn't trust

Nicholas, but his friends were dead unless he gave Nicholas what he wanted. At least then they would have a chance. If something went wrong, maybe Michael and Isabel would find a way to save them.

"Then hurry, Max. In case you haven't noticed, I'm not getting any younger," Nicholas said.

His friends were calling to him, begging him not to. He ignored them. It would just make it harder for him to do what he had to do. Besides, he wasn't through yet. Maybe he could give Nicholas a surprise. But he couldn't do anything while Nicholas held his friends' lives in his hands.

"Now," Nicholas said, approaching him.

"Lie down," Max ordered. Even if this worked, it would be rough for Nicholas. His body was literally falling apart. If he was lying down, he was less likely to drop the remote control.

Nicholas lay down and looked up at Max. Looking down, Max could see that Nicholas was very close to death, maybe closer than Clayton Wheeler had been. Max had been able to restore Wheeler to youth, but doing it had cost Max his own life. He heard Liz's voice, but tried to shut it out. She knew what he was about to do, and what the effort might cost him.

He did not respond. He knew he couldn't if he wanted to keep his resolve and do what he had to do. It might mean he would not have a chance to say good-bye to her—or to any of them—but he had no choice.

Raising his hands, Max took one last look at Nicholas. A full third of his face was gone, and another major part of it was dead already. Nicholas's eyes stared up at him. They were full of malice.

Max didn't want that to be the last thing he saw. He glanced up at his sister, then his friends, and finally Liz. She was calling to him, but he ignored the sound. Instead, he studied her face, taking in every detail. Then Max closed his eyes and put his hands onto Nicholas's body, one on his head and one on his chest. As his hands touched Nicholas, he felt an instant revulsion. Beneath the clothes, Nicholas's flesh did not feel springy as a normal person's would. It felt tough, more like meat than living tissue.

Max knew he could kill him now, channeling his energy to tear apart Nicholas's body, but he knew he would not, because if he did, he would cost his friends any chance they had.

Taking a deep breath, Max concentrated and reached out with his powers, looking for what was wrong with Nicholas's husk. He was surprised to see that the husk was mostly human. Organs and flesh with an alien brain. There was a small, metal device at the base of the spine. That was where the husks were vulnerable, he knew. A blow there and they would literally turn to dust.

Max concentrated on the human portion of the husk, the decaying and dying part of Nicholas. He imagined the damaged parts of the husk healing, rejuvenating. The thought helped, but the process was not one of thought, it was one of will.

He willed the energy that gave him his powers to course through Nicholas's body. As Nicholas had said, his powers were centered in his cerebral cortex. Agent Pierce had said the same thing, and had used drugs to suppress that part of Max's brain. But Max didn't think that either of them had really understood.

Their brains might control the forces they manipulated, but they didn't create them. Something was working through Max, something bigger than the few pounds of tissue in his head. Maybe it was the power of the Granilith, maybe something else. . . .

And right now it was doing its work on the evil person in front of him. *No, not a person, a husk, as skin . . . a thing,* Max thought. But that was all right, if this act saved the others. Max pushed harder. Willed harder. He felt it working.

And he felt it costing him.

He was losing something of himself, some of his power. It happened whenever he healed someone and it usually took some time for him to recover. Still, Max pushed harder, opening himself up. Though his eyes were closed, he could see light coming off Nicholas's body. There were sounds, voices, but he was barely aware of the noise.

As he put more of himself into Nicholas, he saw memory flashes. By now, he recognized them as flashes of home. Max realized he was missing an opportunity here. If he concentrated, he could be probing into Nicholas's mind.

Without breaking the healing connection between them, Max saw Nicholas's malice, his hatred of him and the others. His contempt for humans, and something else . . . ambition. Ambition that went beyond wanting to control one of the five planets.

He saw that Nicholas was telling the truth about the remote control in his hand. His friends would die if Nicholas let go of it. He looked for Nicholas's intentions toward the others. It was hard to see. His mind was full of twists and schemes.

Then Max felt Nicholas push back. Of course, the connection went both ways. Nicholas was getting stronger now, and probing him. He was seeing things, flashes of Max's life. And he was looking for something . . . the Granilith.

Max shut his mind, broke that part of their contact. He was almost certain that Nicholas had not seen the location of the Granilith and was grateful. But what else had he seen? Max felt sick knowing Nicholas had seen inside his mind.

He pushed the thought aside and concentrated on the healing. It was working. Max could feel the energy he controlled doing its job. Nicholas was nearly restored, and Max was weakening. The same process had led to Max's death with Wheeler. But it wasn't going to go that far this time. Max was different from how he had been when he had first healed Liz, different from when he had healed Wheeler.

Max was stronger now.

With a final push, Max allowed his energy to finish its work. Finally, he picked up his hands. Opening his eyes, he saw that Nicholas looked like he did in Copper Summit—like a normal, if creepy, teenage boy. He was healed, and it had taken nearly everything that Max had. Nearly everything . . .

But not *everything*.

Max felt a surge of hope. Maybe this wasn't over. Maybe there was a chance for him to save his friends *and* to defeat Nicholas once and for all. He had just survived something that would have killed him as recently as a year ago, so anything was possible.

Lifting his hands off Nicholas, Max sat back on the floor and took a deep breath. He was sweating and he knew he must look awful. Liz was saying something, asking him if he was okay . . . so were the others. For a second, he couldn't find his voice, so he just raised his hand to signal that he was all right. And he was all right. He wasn't well—he was a long way from that—but he was okay. Hope rose in his chest, faint but there.

He saw Nicholas open his eyes and touch his own face with one hand. Then he looked at Max and smiled.

"You did it," Nicholas said. "And you're still here. The way things felt there, I wasn't sure if you would make it." He got up, jumped to his feet. "You know, Max, I haven't felt this good in fifty years."

Max raised his head slowly; there was no sense in letting Nicholas know that he felt marginally better than he must have looked. Nicholas leaned down to him and grabbed him by the hair, lifting up his face.

"It's a shame you're not up to par. A few minutes ago, it was me who was under the weather. Now, it's you. Feeling weak, Max? Powers gone? Too bad, really. I always wondered who would come out on top if we went *mano a mano,* powers against powers. Oh well . . . ," he said.

"As I recall, you were never much for a fair fight," Max said. It was a guess, but Nicholas twitched and Max could see that he had struck a nerve. Then the moment passed and he smiled. "That's the problem with you, Zan. You only know one way to fight, head on. You never had an appreciation for the value of subtlety, planning, real strategy."

"You mean dirty tricks and backstabbing maneuvers," Max said.

"Six of one hand, Max, half dozen of the other. But I will point out that you are the one who lost his throne and his kingdom and is now on the floor, barely able to sit up while I hold all the cards," Nicholas said.

"You got what you wanted, now let them go," Max said.

"Not yet. You will tell me where the Granilith is first, then you will die," Nicholas said.

"Let them go first," Max said. "You have me."

Nicholas shook his head and said, "Can't do that, but I will show you that you can believe me."

He hit a switch on the remote control and then tossed it aside. For a terrible moment, Max thought he had hit the switch to electrocute Liz and his friends, but nothing happened.

"We can deal, Max. Tell me where it is and I will kill you quickly," Nicholas said.

"Don't do it, Max," Liz said. "Don't tell him anything."

Max looked into Nicholas's eyes and remembered what he had seen when they were connected. Liz was right: He couldn't trust him to keep his word. In fact, if anything, he could depend on Nicholas to break it.

"Okay," he said. "Just let me say good-bye to my friends."

Nicholas nodded, and Max got up, slowly—more slowly than he needed to. He just needed to get close to Nicholas; he needed one chance to make this come out all right. One chance to do right by his friends and by Liz.

Nicholas stepped behind him and grabbed his arm to pull him up, and Max seized the opportunity. He twisted his body so that he was leaning on Nicholas's small, teenaged frame. As he came up, he balled his fist. He heard Nicholas gasp as he realized something was wrong. The husk twisted in his arms, but Max held him firm as he brought his fist down hard and made contact with Nicholas's lower back.

As soon as he felt the contact, Max pushed the husk away from him and waited to see him disappear. For an instant, he saw terror on Nicholas's face, but the instant passed and Nicholas was still there.

Nicholas looked as surprised as Max did. "I think you missed. The spot you were looking for is a little to the right," he said. Nicholas smiled, but there was no humor in it. "You surprised me, Max. That was unusually . . . *sneaky*," Nicholas said.

Max stood as tall and straight as he could and said, "You'll find I'm full of surprises." In a quick motion, he raised his hand and blasted Nicholas as hard as he could. His powers were nowhere near full strength, but they were enough to knock Nicholas off his feet and onto his back. For a second, Max thought the contact with the floor might do the job that his fist had failed to do, but it did not.

Max summoned his powers again and tried for another blast, but before he could release it, Nicholas was on his feet and raising his own hand. He threw out his own force at Max. Instinctively, Max brought up his green shield, which absorbed the impact of the blow. It bowed inward, toward Max, but held. Max could feel his power fading, the shield weakening even as Nicholas increased the power of his own attack.

Concentrating, Max thought of Liz, of Isabel, of Michael, and of their friends. He thought of all their lives, of all his failures, and summoned all the strength he had left.

And it wasn't enough.

The shields crackled brightly and then disappeared. Max's hand fell to his side, then he crumbled to the floor.

"You're just making me angry!" Nicholas said. But he wasn't just angry, Max saw. He was scared. Max saw that he had surprised and scared Nicholas. How close had Max come to destroying him with those blows? *Pretty close,* he thought. *But not close enough.*

"You just don't know when you're beaten," Nicholas said. "I guess I'll have to show you."

Max felt an unseen force grab him and push him backward. He was sliding away from Nicholas. Curled into a ball, Max wondered how far he was from the rear wall of the room. A second later, he didn't have to wonder. He crashed into it, taking the impact first with his back, then with his head.

The pain was sudden and intense.

Then he was sliding back the other way. He could see the other wall looming.

"Stop it," Isabel said. "I'll tell you where the Granilith is. Just don't hurt him."

Suddenly Max felt the hold on him disappear, and he was lying on the floor in front of Nicholas.

Max raised his head and tried to say *no,* but his mouth wouldn't work. Nicholas approached Isabel and said, "So tell me."

"You have to let Max go," she said.

He shook his head, "No, I don't. See, before morning, I'm going to kill him and throw him in the freezer upstairs until Kevar arranges for me to be picked up. Before that happens you will have given me the Granilith." Isabel started to protest, but Nicholas silenced her with a wave. "When I go to work on you and your friends, you'll tell me anything I want to know. Then I'll kill you and by then you'll be begging me to do it."

No! Max's mind screamed. He tried to push himself off the floor, but his body wouldn't cooperate.

Nicholas leaned down to him and whispered, "You failed them again, Max. Your sister, Michael, your friends, especially your girlfriend. And before you die, I want you to know that I am going to enjoy myself with your women. After all, you brought me back to health, and a person my age has needs. I will enjoy getting reacquainted with your sister. And I look forward to getting to know your current mate."

Pushing off the floor, Max lunged at Nicholas, who moved away easily. Max lay on the floor, panting. He had failed them, and his failure was much worse than he had feared.

It was over, Max felt it.

18

Liz watched Max lying on the floor. He had given every-thing to his fight with Nicholas, and now he looked barely alive. He had sacrificed so much for all of them. He had taken on so many burdens and blamed himself for so much. And he had suffered so much at the hands of evil people. First Agent Pierce, now Nicholas. It was too much for him, and it was too much for her to watch, but she refused to look away.

Then he turned his head and looked at her, mouthing the words "I'm sorry." She knew he blamed himself for some perceived failure, as if all of their fates were his per-sonal responsibility, that all of their lives rested on his shoulders.

She wanted to tell him that it wasn't true. That this was the life they had all chosen, this was the life *she* had cho-sen. This fight was all of theirs. And this defeat was all of theirs as well.

In the end, all she could do was look at him and whis-per back, "It's okay, Max." She tried to communicate the rest with her eyes. She wanted to make this part easier for him, to comfort him, but she could tell by his eyes that she had not.

That was her failure, and her shame.

"Okay?" Nicholas snapped, suddenly in front of her. "You think this is okay. If by all right, you mean pain and death for all of you, then yes, I'd say this is all just fine."

Looking into his sneering face, Liz knew what it was like to truly hate someone. He had won, and he was still trying to scare them, to torture them, to hurt Max through her and them. In her fury, she pulled at the straps that held her arms to the wall behind her at her waist. She couldn't break them. In fact, she couldn't even budge them. All she could do was stomp her feet in her anger.

Her feet.

They were free. She was bound to the wall, but she could still move her feet, and Nicholas had made the mistake of getting very close to her, to frighten her more. Without a moment's hesitation, she brought a single foot up with all of her might, aiming it where she knew it would hurt most. It hit with a satisfying thud, and Nicholas looked at her in shock and pain. Then he crumbled into a ball on the ground.

Liz felt a flash of satisfaction. She had fought back, even if just for a moment. And she had hurt him, pretty badly by the sound of his moaning. It might be their last victory of the day, and in the end it wouldn't make a real difference, but Liz smiled at the sight.

She only wished she could have fought harder and made a real difference. Thinking back to her dream-vision of the future, she remembered seeing Michael and Isabel lying dead while Max stood alone to battle some monstrous force. Even then he was trying to protect her, but the force he was facing was too great.

And then he had died for her . . . for all of them.

Was that vision about *this* fight, with the metaphor of dreams replacing Nicholas with a monster? It seemed impossible. Nicholas was too small and petty to be the force that finally destroyed Max.

Liz felt now like she had felt in the vision: an observer, helpless. She could not fight, had not fought then. How could she? She had powers, but she couldn't control them. Her visions had helped them before, and her other powers had helped Max in Stonewall, but she couldn't even summon them now.

All she had been able to muster was a swift kick against a monster in the body of a small, skinny, teenaged boy. Even drained by his healing of Nicholas, Max had managed more than that. If she somehow survived, if some miracle saved all of them, Liz vowed to develop and master her powers.

If only she had done that sooner, if only she could fight like Max, or Michael, or Isabel. She could make books burst into flame and occasionally move objects, but that was nothing against Nicholas and his abilities. If only . . .

Looking across the room to Michael's and Kyle's pained faces, Liz knew that she wasn't the only one feeling helpless. Michael could do it, if he was free, if it wasn't for the electrodes blocking his powers.

Liz realized that if even she was able to get herself and her hands free for a few seconds, she would be able to rip them from Michael's head. Then she knew that he would do the rest—the look on his face told her that. Her hands were incapacitated, but what if she could do it without her hands? She had moved objects before, even under stress. And this would not require the same power as a full-blown fight against Nicholas's alien powers. This would just require a nudge with her own infant abilities . . . just a nudge.

She looked at Michael, concentrating on the electrodes. She saw that he was saying something to Maria, trying to comfort her. She blocked out the noise, all noise, and concentrated on the electrodes on each side of his forehead. They were attached by a device that looked like a set of metal headphones. Even so, they were light, she was sure, less than a pound. She focused. Did the headset move slightly? She wasn't sure, but she thought it might have.

That's when she felt a slap across her face, shattering her concentration. She was annoyed at the interruption. Then she saw Nicholas standing there and realized what it meant: He had recovered enough to stand up. And he was angry.

He was standing to the side, out of the range of her foot. Leaning in, he whispered, "That was a mistake. You're going to regret that. I had wanted to save you for last, to give Max plenty of time to think about what was going to happen to you, but now you will die first."

The words barely registered. She was trying to regain her concentration on Michael's headset. If she could only move it, there still might be a chance. Nicholas was pulling her, releasing her arms, then gripping them firmly from behind. Maria was crying loudly now, and Isabel was saying something. So were Kyle and Michael. She ignored all the words and concentrated on the headset.

The headset. Suddenly she could feel it in her mind. Its metal warmed by Michael's skin. She felt its weight.

Nicholas was talking. To her? No, to Max. Then she was falling, thrown to the floor next to Max. Looking up, she saw Nicholas looming over her. He was taunting Max and trying to frighten her, but she could think only of the headset.

Lifting his own foot, Nicholas kicked Max squarely in the stomach, and she watched her boyfriend shudder at the blow. She felt a rush of adrenaline and feeling for Max.

That did it.

Suddenly, she was holding the headset with her mind, as firmly as if she were holding it with her hand. In the end, it seemed painfully simple. All she had to do was . . . *yank*. And then it was flying across the room.

"Michael, now!" she called out. Then she reached out again with her mind, felt the straps holding Michael to the chamber. She broke them with her mind. Then, as quickly as they had come, her powers began to recede—like a dream that races out of sight when you wake.

It was all right. Michael could take it from here, and right now, Max needed her.

As Michael stumbled out of his chamber, a change came over Nicholas's face. His sneering grin disappeared, only to be replaced by a look of dull surprise. "What . . . ," he said feebly.

"Now you're going to pay," Michael said, raising his hand. Liz realized it would soon be over. Nicholas was too confused to mount a defense. And Michael was angry. His face had a kind of determined fury that she had never seen on him before. She knew how he felt about Max and how he must have felt about what had happened here for the last few minutes.

Liz decided she wouldn't want to be Nicholas right now.

His brow furrowed in concentration, Michael summoned his powers. Then he pushed with his outstretched hand and . . .

Nothing.

Surprise registered on Michael's face. He tried again. This time, Nicholas stumbled back slightly, as if he had been pushed gently. Looking at Nicholas's face, Liz saw that his dumb look of shock was gone, and the sneering grin was back.

"Oh Michael, you know there might be some residual effects from the electrode," he said, then he laughed. The sound was less unnatural than it had been when he was a walking, rotting corpse, but it was no less creepy.

Liz raced to Max and instinctively put her body over his, holding him. It was an empty gesture, she knew. Once again, she was helpless.

"Watch this, Max. This will give you some idea of what to expect for yourself." Nicholas raised his hand, pointing it at Michael. The hand began to glow, and Maria screamed. Something happened. Liz could hear a thump and realized that Nicholas must have hit Michael with his energy.

She didn't even turn around. Instead, she found herself getting up. Nicholas was just in front of and to the side of her. She didn't really have a plan, just her own rage. For the moment, it felt like enough.

She threw herself into him, driving him toward one of the empty chambers. Though he might have been a powerful and evil alien on the inside, on the outside he was just a little over her own height. What happened next was physics.

Nicholas went flying into the closed glass chamber, which shattered on impact. Liz fell to the floor as Nicholas fell into the glass. She was on her feet nearly instantly and grabbed Nicholas as he started to get up himself. Just as she had grabbed Maria on the stairs, she grabbed Nicholas by the back of his jeans and swung him around with all of her might.

Already off balance, Nicholas went flying toward the chamber on the other side of the narrow room. He went into it face first, and that one shattered as well. Besides the glass, Liz saw blood splattering. For a moment, she hoped he had cut something vital, but he got up too quick for that to be true.

When he turned to look up at her, Liz could see a deep cut across his face that went from the right side of his forehead, down through the bridge of his nose, and deeply into his left cheek. She had hurt him, but not fatally.

When he spoke, it was to her. "You're just like Zan here—you don't know when you're beaten." He shook his head, and the remote control caught his eye. His arm flung out as he dove for it.

Liz realized there was no time to reach it before he did, so she did the only thing she could. Lifting her foot, she raised it quickly and brought it down hard on the remote—just as Nicholas's hand was reaching the device. She felt the remote crack under her heel as his fingers reached under the front of her shoe.

He gave a yelp and pulled his hand back. Liz brought her foot down again on the remote, then lifted it to see that it was in a number of very small pieces. *So much for high-tech alien weapons,* she thought.

Nicholas got up slowly and raised his hand in her direction. Turning her eyes from Nicholas, Liz looked at Max lying on the floor. She felt a swell of feeling for him and took a snapshot of him in her mind, ready to take it with her into her end.

Looking at Max, Liz could only see what happened next with her peripheral vision. Suddenly, Nicholas was flying backward through the air. Turning her head, she saw him land heavily on the floor and continue sliding back toward the doorway. Then he was outside, and the door shut behind him.

When Liz turned again, she saw Michael standing with his hand out. Isabel and Maria were climbing out of their chambers, and Liz realized that Michael must have freed them. Isabel rubbed her head as Maria ran to Michael and wrapped her arms around him.

He kept his hand up and said, evenly, "Everyone get behind me, and grab Max."

Then there was pounding on the heavy metal door. Liz didn't turn to look; she grabbed Max by one shoulder and pulled. Maria and Isabel reached down to help her. Together, they pulled him several feet behind Michael, who was straining with the effort of holding Nicholas back. The door was bowing inward. Isabel stood next to him and raised her own hand. "Sorry, Michael. Nothing," she said.

"Just give it a minute," he said, the strain clear in his voice.

Then there was the wrenching sound of tearing metal, and the door broke from its hinges and flew toward them. With a final push, Michael forced it to the ground. The door still came toward them, but it slowed gradually until it stopped nearly at Michael's feet.

"So it comes down to you and me, Kevar's second in command and Zan's. The problem is that I'm guessing you're still a little underpowered from my electrodes," Nicholas said, blood running freely down his face.

Liz could see muscle underneath the deep cut in his cheek. Once again, he looked like the monster he was.

"I've got more than enough juice to put you down, you pathetic little twerp," Michael said. His voice was firm, but Liz knew he was pushing his limits. She tried to summon her own meager powers, but couldn't.

Nicholas lifted his hand, and his energy flew across the room. Michael seemed to recoil for a moment, then he held firm. Both of them were hurling their energy at each other—a bright flash in the center of the room indicated where their energy met. It was dead center between the two of them. For now, the forces seemed to be canceling each other out.

The effort was taking a toll on both of them, Liz could see from Nicholas's face and the tense strain in Michael's body. Liz leaned down to hold Max, not looking away. She could see that Michael was fighting for them all now, and fighting with everything he had. But he was losing.

The air in the room changed and the collision between Michael and Nicholas's force was moved closer to Michael.

Then it was over. Something snapped, and Michael went flying back. "No!" Maria screamed, running to him.

Nicholas kept coming. "That's it, I've had it with all of you." He threw out his hand, but nothing happened. Confused, he tried again, but Isabel had recovered enough to put up a fight against him. Nicholas was openly surprised. "Vilandra, this isn't like you. You were never much of a fighter. Parties were more your style," he said.

"Things change," she said, hitting him with enough force to send him reeling several steps back.

"Don't think I'm going to take it easy on you," he said, hurling energy back at her. She repelled it easily, then hit him again. He staggered back.

Then again.

And again.

He was forced almost to the ruined doorway. He stood his ground there, as Isabel hit him hard. Nicholas flew backward and then onto the floor on the landing outside. Surprise turned to dismay on his face as he looked up at Isabel and got to his feet, then he turned quickly and disappeared up the stairs.

"Stay with the guys," Isabel said to Liz and Maria. "He's mine."

19

Isabel ran up the stairs to the basement. She heard noise from the stairs leading up to the ground level of the house and took the stairs two at a time, then three. She was taller than Nicholas and had no doubt she was faster. If he tried to run on open ground, she knew she would have him. She quickly made her way through the basement and up another set of stairs.

She burst through the door into the kitchen and heard footsteps heading toward the front of the house. Isabel followed, heading through hallways and rooms until she stepped into the great room. Looking ahead at the front door, she saw that it was closed. She hadn't heard it open or close, so she figured Nicholas was still in the house, somewhere.

Her anger fueled her as she focused on the fact that Nicholas had tried to kill Max, her friends, and then kill her. He had wanted to bring death to this house.

More death, she thought.

The Bentons had all died here. But they had been the

victims of a mindless sickness. She and her friends would have been the victims of Nicholas's *purpose,* a purpose as dark as anything she could imagine.

Then she heard another noise coming from the back of the house. She was in the kitchen seconds later, following the noise. She crossed the room quickly and threw open the door to the infirmary. Nicholas spun around to face her, and she could see that he had knocked several trays to the ground. His face was covered in blood, and he looked unsteady on his feet.

Isabel didn't hesitate, she raised her hand and hit him with everything she had. He responded quickly and met her force with his own. There was a bright flash between them, and for a long moment it was a stalemate. Nicholas broke the silence. "Vilandra, it doesn't have to end like this. If we both go to Kevar with the Granilith—"

"Stop!" she said. "It's going to end right now. I'm going to see that you never hurt anyone again." Isabel pushed harder, reaching out with her mind and her will.

Nicholas met the attack. "Face it, Vilandra, you're just not a fighter. You really should leave that sort of thing to your brother, Zan, and his pathetic second."

She thought of Max, fighting for her. Gentle Max, who as a small boy had once healed a bird with a broken wing before he'd even known he had the ability to heal. And it was not an accident that Max could heal, that that was his special ability. He was good, better than she was. When they were younger, she had resented that, afraid that her parents and everyone else could see it.

Now she just wanted to protect Max, who had risked his entire existence to save an innocent girl who had been shot in a diner, who had spent his whole life trying to protect Isabel. She had never quite believed that she deserved what he gave her freely.

Max was better than her, and stronger. Every time he healed someone, he gave them some part of his power. And every time he did it, it made him stronger. That paradox was the secret of Max's strength. Suddenly, she felt petty and selfish. She had complained and whined for too long about her desire for a normal life. Max had long ago put away those desires and concentrated on protecting her and Michael. And then the friends that had joined their circle.

"Vilandra, it's time—," Nicholas began.

"My name's not Vilandra, it's Isabel. And you hurt my brother, you son of a bitch," Isabel said, reaching out with her weakened powers. For a moment, she had more strength than she'd ever had, and she imagined what it must feel like for Max—to do something for someone else, to draw power from that effort.

But it was for just a moment. Nicholas recoiled, then recovered and saw the point of the collision of their energies begin to shift from the middle of the room . . . and toward her.

Max had fallen, then Liz had tried, then Michael. Nicholas was too strong, and it disgusted her to know that he had taken most of the strength he carried from her brother's healing touch. Isabel knew her own strength would fail in a moment and there would be no one left to pick up the fight.

Death would come again to this house. It seemed . . . unfair. Isabel thought of the Bentons, living, laughing, loving, and then dying here. Then there was a subtle shift in the energy of the room again. Suddenly Isabel had the feeling that she and Nicholas weren't alone anymore. She had had the feeling before in this house, and she knew where it came from . . . she *felt* where it came from.

They were not alone. The house was still full of life. It had always been full, even in the dark days since a mother and children had succumbed to a terrible disease here, since a father had grieved here. They had all left something of themselves in this place.

Isabel felt her strength return, then grow. The tide of the battle was changing again, and Isabel knew she wasn't the one doing it. Someone understood what Nicholas was, and didn't want him in this house.

With a single burst, Isabel pushed with all of her will and there was an explosion of light that illuminated the room. Before it could dim, she could see Nicholas flying backward, across the room and through the great windows and the sheet of plastic that covered them.

Then it was silent, and the room was dim.

She felt exhausted and was tempted to just let herself fall to the floor, but she had to make sure. . . .

Isabel stumbled to the open window and saw the place where Nicholas had landed on the ground. The overgrown grass was bent down, but he was gone. Then she saw his dark figure stagger across the field toward the garage and it disappeared.

She considered going after him, but Isabel knew she would not get far, so she just stood and waited. A few seconds later, headlights that illuminated the darkness and an SUV crashed through the gate its way out. The taillights faded as it headed down the road.

Nicholas was still alive, but she knew he wouldn't bother them again tonight, or anytime soon. Though she was sure they would see him again, she had the feeling that he would never return to this house. Had he felt the other presence in the room? Had he felt its judgment?

It was crazy to think it, but Isabel was certain that it was true. She had had help in her fight against Nicholas, in her fight for the only family she had ever known. And that help had come from someone who knew something about loss and had seen enough of death.

Unable to stand anymore, Isabel felt herself drift down to the hospital bed nearby. Then she closed her eyes and slept.

Sometime later, someone came to get her. Strong arms picked her up off the bed and carried her to another bed. It might have been Max, or Michael, or Kyle. She wasn't sure, but it was someone who cared for her.

It was one of her family.

20

It was less than four hours until sunup, and more than once in that time, Liz was not sure that Max was going to make it. There were cuts and scrapes on his body, but they were superficial. His problems were deeper, impossible for her to see. He was hot, and she knew that was not good for him. Healing Nicholas—bringing that monster back from the brink of death—and then fighting him had cost Max a part of himself.

Isabel and Michael were depleted as well, but Liz saw that they would be all right. Isabel slept peacefully in the double bed next to Max's. Her color was good, and Liz did not think there was anything wrong with her that rest would not cure.

Michael was another story. He didn't have much strength, and he had a number of cuts and bruises, including a long and deep one on his back. Max would be able to take care of them easily, if he recovered. When *he recovers*, Liz thought. She couldn't help but think of the irony of the situation: The person best able to help someone in Max's condition was Max, but he could not heal himself—at least not until he was awake, and himself again.

During the few remaining hours of night, Michael had insisted on sitting up and watching over Max and Isabel, which he did from a large, winged-back chair near the door. *He's standing guard,* Liz had realized. Maria sat on the floor, resting on Michael's leg. She was standing guard, too, Liz saw. Maria had thrown a blanket over Michael and had brought him food, which he refused, and water, which he took. Kyle had paced continually, never straying far from Isabel.

Liz tried to keep Max cool with cold compresses, and by the time the first rays of light shone through the window, his temperature was normal. He was still unconscious, but he would take small sips of water through his dry lips, and Liz started to relax. By the time the sun was up fully, Max's color was back to normal, and he seemed to be only sleeping.

When that happened, Michael finally fell asleep in the chair. They had tried to move him a number of times, but he had shaken them off. Finally, they left him in the chair. Then Maria climbed into the chair next to him and fell asleep there as well.

"Why don't you get some sleep, Liz," Kyle suggested. "He's going to be fine," he added, gesturing to Max.

Liz nodded and climbed under the blanket that now covered Max. Within seconds she was asleep, and she didn't wake again until it was dark. By then, Isabel was up and she, Liz, and Maria managed to maneuver Michael into the other bed. A couple of hours later, Michael woke up.

Max slept through the night again. Liz fell asleep some-time later. In the morning, Liz felt something on her face. A soft touch. Her eyes opened and saw Max looking down on her, smiling. Then he kissed her. She gave in to the kiss, then broke away to examine him. He looked a little worn and still tired, but he was alive. Liz clutched him tightly and said a silent prayer of thanks.

"I'm okay, Liz. I'm okay," he said, then he kissed her again.

Maria's voice broke the moment. "Okay, break it up, no public displays in the creepy old mansion."

Liz smiled and looked at her friend. Maria was beam-ing. She was also dressed and clean. So were Isabel, Kyle, and Michael. And so was Max, for that matter. Both his and Michael's cuts were gone, and Liz assumed that Max had healed them. He really was better—almost himself, she could see.

"Come on, Parker," Maria said. "Chop, chop, we don't get out of here until you get yourself ready."

"Actually, I was thinking we could stay a while, at least another day," Isabel said.

"Why?" Michael asked.

Isabel was quiet for a moment, then she said, "Gee, I don't know. Let's see, spend the next day and night in a stinky old van with five other people, or stay in a mansion stocked with food and drink."

"Yeah, but—," Maria started to say.

"We should have a party. This place was built for par-ties," Isabel said.

"What if he comes back?" Michael asked.

"He won't, I'm sure of it," Isabel said.

"Maybe we should vote on it," Max said.

"Sorry Max, this isn't a democracy," Isabel said.

"I guess it's a party, then," Michael said.

Isabel spent the morning going through the house and using her powers to clean up and repair the damage done from the night before. She wanted to erase any sign that Nicholas had been here. She found two cast-iron pokers imbedded in the hallway walls upstairs. Then there was the infirmary, which she hadn't wanted to enter at first.

Inside, she found that the room didn't give her the bad feeling it had the first time she had seen it. It just seemed empty now, and peaceful. She repaired the broken window easily and picked up the few things that had been displaced.

She thought the Bentons would approve.

Isabel went down to the basement and stood there for a long time before she walked through the door and down the staircase into the sub-basement. She considered getting Max or Michael to come with her, but she didn't think she could explain to them why she was doing what she was about to do.

In the end, she had steeled herself and walked quickly down the stairs. Inside the lab, she summoned her powers and went to work. She melted all of the equipment and pods, fusing them into unrecognizable masses of rubble. For a moment, she worried that she might be giving the Special Unit something to study. Then she realized that when she was finished, they would know less about what happened here if they came looking, not more.

She wished she could fill in the space, but she had to satisfy herself with destroying everything that he had brought into this house. Stepping back into the basement, she pulled concrete from the surrounding walls to cover up the place where the door had been. Now, no one could tell anything had ever been there.

Then she turned and headed upstairs. In the kitchen, the others were getting ready to cook. Michael carried in some frozen meat from the walk-in freezer. Kyle brought in armfuls of food from the pantry.

"I don't want to speculate on your friends the Skins' diet and biology, but Nicholas sure did pack a lot of beans. I mean, you wouldn't believe it," he said.

They all laughed, even Isabel, and the laughter felt good. It belonged in this house. They spent the afternoon cooking and set the table with china and crystal that had been lovingly maintained but not used in many years, Isabel guessed. Michael had wanted them to use their powers to prepare the food. Isabel refused to allow it. Though it was quicker, it never tasted the same.

After their meal, they gathered around the fire in the great room. The boys had found some snacks and they had talked and laughed. Then Maria began to play the guitar and sing.

Isabel lost track of time. It was a party, a real party with friends who felt at home with one another in a place that was beautiful and *comfortable*. As the night drew to a close, Isabel had the feeling that there were five more guests at the party, five people she and her friends couldn't see.

Isabel imagined that three of those people were up past their bedtime, but had gotten special permission from their parents. When the fire finally went out, Isabel said a silent thanks to the Bentons and headed up the stairs.

• • •

"Okay Max," open your eyes," Liz said, and Max did. She was once again wearing her new black nightgown.

He smiled. "Nice surprise," he said, unable to take his eyes off of her.

"I take it that the king approves?" she said.

"Liz, I'm not the king," he replied. "I'm nobody's leader."

"You're mine, you're all of ours," she countered.

"Your visions have told you how that's going to turn out," he said.

"No, Max, it's not. We're going to change that. *You're* going to change that," she said.

"How? I couldn't save you from Nicholas. In fact, it was you, and Michael, and Isabel . . . ," he said, feeling flush with the memory of his failure.

"No, Max, we helped, and you gave us that chance. It's not all about you, you know," she said.

"I thought I was king," he teased.

Then Liz's face became serious. "Like it or not, Max, you're the leader of this group, and part of that leadership is to let some of us do something once in a while. You can't put it all on your shoulders. It's not fair to you, or to us." Max started to argue, but she shushed him. "You said it yourself once: You have to use your powers more. You're stronger than you were when I met you. All three of you are."

"What about you?" he asked. He had seen some of what she did, and Michael had told him the rest.

"Even me," she said, and added, "I'll help out when I can." She was amazing. She had saved them all by freeing

Michael and keeping Nicholas off balance long enough for Michael and Isabel to recover.

"I guess that makes you the power behind the throne," he said. She smiled again—brightly, brilliantly, beautifully. "That makes you queen," he said.

Her smile turned coy. "Would you deny your queen anything?"

He shook his head.

She pulled him closer and said, "Then I have my first royal request."

"Yes, ma'am," he said, and then he kissed her.

"You know, Spaceboy, you just proved my point," Maria said as they entered the bedroom.

"What?" he said, already not liking her tone. As usual, it had come out of nowhere.

"What do you mean, "what"? You and Nicholas, *mano a mano*, throwing yourself in front of trouble," she said, shaking her head. "This is just the kind of thing I was talking about. You're Sonny Corleone, a walking time bomb."

"Well, I mean, what was I supposed to do?" Michael sputtered.

"You're supposed to stay out of trouble," she said.

Michael felt the hair on the back of his neck prick up as the blood rushed to his face. "In case you weren't paying attention, he was going to kill all of us. That's the kind of trouble that's hard to avoid. And what about you? What about taking an iron poker and trying to brain him with it? At least I have powers," he said.

"That was completely different," she said, with an air of finality.

"How?" he demanded.

"It just was," she said.

"Look Maria, everybody dies, but not everybody—"

"Don't!" she shouted at him. "Don't give me that macho crap."

"Look, I don't want to lose you. I'm not going to let anyone hurt you, ever, if I can help it," he said.

Maria paused, and then threw her arms around him. "I thought I was going to lose you," she said.

He held her quietly for a long moment and then whispered, "You're not going to get rid of me that easily."

Pulling back, he looked at her and wiped the tears from her face. "Look Maria, everybody does die, but not everybody has a girl like you. In fact, I'm the only one, and I'm not going to let anyone get in the way of that. If that means taking out the odd alien in human form, then so be it. But whatever happens, you are not getting rid of me."

"Michael," she said softly, then she kissed him. A moment later, she pulled away and disappeared into the bathroom. When she emerged, she was wearing something black, and small.

Very small.

"Wow," was all he could say.

"It's a surprise," she said. "For you."

"But I didn't get you anything," he replied, approaching her. Then she was in his arms, and he felt himself getting lost.

"You'll have to make it up to me, then," she said.

EPILOGUE

After Isabel stowed her things in the van, she went back into the master bedroom and found the journal on the floor beside the bed. Picking it up, she placed it carefully on the shelf with the others.

She wondered why Robert Benton had shown it to her—she no longer doubted that that was exactly what had happened. Had he wanted her to know their story? Had he tried to warn her? To tell her something? She wasn't sure, but she was glad he had done it.

The upstairs was empty, and she walked through the family's bedrooms, lingering in Sarah's room, where the rocking horse sat. *They were here,* she realized. They were still in this house, together now, and it was a good place to be.

Comfortable, she thought. *And happy.*

But there was just one more thing she had to do, and she knew she had to hurry; the others would be ready soon. She headed out the back door, and into the backyard, though *grounds* was a more accurate word.

She walked in the field for a short time, explored it for a few minutes. Then she saw a grassy hill to the side. On a hunch, she walked over to it.

At the top near a large shade tree she found what she was looking for. There were five headstones. She read the dates. Four of them were decades old. One was much newer. There it was, the proof of everything she had thought and felt about this house and the people who had lived in it.

But she had not needed proof. She had merely wanted to understand something. To say thank you to Robert Benton, who she now knew had no doubt saved her life and the lives of all of her friends. Isabel fell to her knees on the ground in front of the graves, in the wildflowers that grew on this hill but apparently nowhere else that she could see.

That did not surprise her. In fact, it made its own sense in the way this house made its own sense.

The tears came suddenly, and Isabel did not try to stop them. She cried for a mother and her children who had been taken by disease. She cried for a father who had lost everything but the memory of his family—a memory that had had to sustain him for fifty years of life alone in an empty house.

She cried for herself and the life she had left behind in Roswell. She cried for her parents and for Jesse who had loved her and whom she had loved. Then she did something she had not done since she had lost him. Isabel cried for Alex, who had been a better person than she was and who had died too soon. He had died before she could tell him anything, before she could give him what he wanted from her and what he had deserved.

As the ground soaked up her tears, she remembered what he had said to her: "It's getting late."

Late for her? Late for him?

Isabel wasn't sure what the answer was. She guessed that part of it was that she needed to let him go. Was that one of the things Robert Benton was trying to communicate? Isabel knew she wasn't ready, but she also knew the time would come.

Though the tears had started abruptly, they ended slowly. Finally, she heard voices calling her name and she rose to her feet. She took a last look at the Bentons' final resting place, then turned to walk down the hill.

She saw them all waiting for her by the van. There was music, loud music, coming from the van.

Michael and his heavy metal, she thought, shaking her head.

She brushed away a final tear and then heard Kyle say, "Come on, Stinky Van Express is about to pull out."

Isabel smiled. Then she ran to join her friends.

ABOUT THE AUTHOR

Kevin Ryan is the author of the Roswell book *A New Beginning*. He has also written three novels for the best-selling Star Trek series and cowritten another. In addition, Kevin has published a number of comic books and has written for television. He lives in New York with his wife and four children, and can be reached at Kryan1964@aol.com.

**As many as one in three
Americans with HIV...
DO NOT KNOW IT.**

**More than half of those
who will get HIV this year...
ARE UNDER 25.**

**HIV is preventable.
You can help fight AIDS.
Get informed. Get the facts.**

**www.knowhivaids.org
1-866-344-KNOW**

"Well, we could grind our
enemies into powder with a
sledgehammer, but gosh,
we did that last night."

—Xander

As long as there have been vampires,
there has been the Slayer. One girl
in all the world, to find them where
they gather and to stop the spread of
their evil...the swell of their numbers.

LOOK FOR A NEW TITLE
EVERY MONTH!

Based on the hit TV series created by

Joss Whedon

2400

Everyone's got his demons....

ANGEL™

If it takes an eternity, he will make amends.

Original stories based
on the TV show
Created by Joss Whedon
& David Greenwalt

Available from Simon Pulse
Published by Simon & Schuster

SIMON
PULSE